D1824686

THE FIVE YEAR TRIP

RAISTIN SKELLEY

Team Hate Press

For:
Bourdain
Chandler
Heller
Herr
Moore
Pynchon
Steinbeck
Vonnegut
Wambaugh

"You can't be cooler than the corners
where you source all your parts"

-Aesop Rock

THE FIVE YEAR TRIP

CONTENTS

One
Tomorrow Morning   1

Two
Life During Wartime   5

Three
Californian Hills   15

Four
Peace Frog   31

Five
What's He Building?   57

Six
Body Reprise   65

Seven
No Splash   69

Eight
Macombs Dam Bridge   79

Nine
Southbound Pachyderm   83

Ten
Sneakin' Out the Hospital   99

Eleven
Hangover 1/1/83   117

Twelve
Car Thief   137

Thirteen
Elastic Heart   153

Fourteen
Snake Eyes   175

Fifteen
Homework   183

Sixteen
Blue Orchid/Party of Special Things to Do   209

Seventeen
Padam Padam   229

Eighteen
How Far Can Too Far Go?   233

If it keeps on rainin' levee's goin' to break
If it keeps on rainin' levee's goin' to break
And the water gon' come I have no place to stay
Well all last night I sat on the levee and moan
Well all last night I sat on the levee and moan
Thinkin' bout my baby and my happy home
If it keeps on rainin' levee's goin' to break
If it keeps on rainin' levee's goin' to break
And all these people will have no place to stay
Now look here mamma what am I to do?
Now look here mamma what am I to do?
I ain't got nobody to tell my troubles to
I worked on the levee mamma both night and day
I worked on the levee mamma both night and day
I ain't got nobody to keep the water away
Oh cryin' won't help you, prayin' won't do no good
Oh cryin' won't help you, prayin' won't do no good
Whenever the levee breaks mamma you got to lose
I worked on the levee mamma both night and day
I worked on the levee mamma both night and day
I worked so hard to keep the water away
I had a woman she wouldn't do for me
I had a woman she wouldn't do for me
I'm going back to my used to be
Oh mean old levee cause me to weep and moan
Yeah mean old levee cause me to weep and moan
Told me leave my baby and my happy home

- When the Levee Breaks
Kansas Joe McCoy & Memphis Minnie (1929)
Chapter One: Tomorrow Morning

CHAPTER ONE

Tomorrow Morning

Tripper Mayhew's decision to go into work that day was based solely on self-preservation. If he had his druthers he would have stayed at home and avoided the internet for the foreseeable future. But that would have shown weakness and weakness in the face of what seems like virtually colossal adversity isn't taken lightly by co-workers, no matter the work environment. In an office, it breeds doubt and resentment that will ultimately culminate in your termination in about three weeks' time. One week to let it go away, one week to see if it will change, and another week for all the partners to meet and schedule the most convenient day to fire you.

The ballots were in and nobody was happy. Nobody in the offices of LMJ Engineering at least. The most vocal of supporters sat uncomfortably in their broken swivel office chairs and shifted their eyes like cartoon bandits. They say the night is blackest just before the dawn. It was going to be four years before anyone saw sunlight again..

Tripper exchanged angry dumbfounded glances with his desk neighbor Kevin Baird as he sat down. They were on the same page and at that point that was all that really mattered. Tripper opened an ArcGIS file and began surfing around it aimlessly trying to look hard at work while he watched the slow trickle of employees come in. LMJ was not a large company; it employed thirty-five people with varying levels of Civil and Electrical engineering degrees and a handful of licensed surveyors. Tripper's desk was on the first floor, also referred to as "upstairs", and his half of the building sat eight CAD operators including him and all four partners had offices that ran the length of the hall leading to the CAD Room.

After a few minutes of hostile silence, Tripper saw an email icon appear in the bottom right hand corner of his first monitor. It was an email from Kevin:

"Heard any good jokes lately?"

Tripper replied: "Yeah, but the way you have to tell it is pretty NSFW."

Kevin sent a GIF from *Team America* with puppets shaking their heads and crying with laughter. That was something that Tripper had admired about Kevin in the year he'd known him since starting at LMJ, he never really seemed to be down about anything. He could tell Kevin that his own mother died, and Kevin would grin, shake his head and say, 'What are you going to do?'

Just then the bell on the front door in the lobby crashed hard against the plate glass door and jingled violently as the voice of Hunter Musgrave addressed the entire office at once:

"He did it! My boy Donny! He did it! Things are finally looking up! First time in eight years!"

Tripper's eyes quickly darted around the office, examining the re-action of other known supporters. You could hear the water heater kick on in the supply closet of the men's bathroom. Tripper looked back at his screen.

Outside, the grey sky of November hung ominously over the tri-county area. The sky itself had taken on an air of menace, like it had slipped on a samurai mask in the night. The brush that surrounded LMJ rattled as if inhabited by the pre-cognitive ghosts of snipers yet to take position. The freeway that abutted the rear parking lot which was normally nothing more than a sixty-foot high annoy-ance now stood as a castle wall that poured the discordant sounds of traffic down on the office like hot tar. The incoming airplanes that screamed over head, destined to land at the nearby international airport were covered in exterior dome cameras, staring down at the people, vehicles and businesses below, gathering reconnaissance to deliver to unknown persons of power. Every building within a five-hundred-foot radius had a rifleman posted on the roof, and a shad-owy figure with binoculars on the first-floor peering through the venetians. The two hotels three hundred yards east of the office were booked full with members of the FBI and CIA going through the red envelopes in their briefcases as they glanced out their win-dows and ate room service. Overnight the country had been flooded with government agents, covert operatives, plainclothes detectives and Russian sleeper agents. There was no need to draw attention to it. Everyone felt it happen.

One nation, under paranoia.

CHAPTER TWO

Life During Wartime

Office summers are notoriously slow. As are office autumns. What is unexpected is when winter is slow. Usually, contractors are scrambling to finish paper work before the start of the New Year and end up hammering engineers, project managers and ultimately the draftsmen with deadlines so ridiculous a person either snaps or considers developing a serious chemical dependency to deal with the stress. The previous winter had been slow for work. An anomaly for sure, but the thing that annoyed the fuck out of Tripper was the yearlong insistence from project managers that "there's work comin'. In about two weeks."

They say that when you are just starting out in Hollywood, you die two weeks at a time. Two weeks from your first screen test, audition, script pitch, what have you. From an outsider's point of view that does seem to be the case. Unless you are conventionally attractive or have the fellatio skills of a college art history professor's star student, in which case you will be directing and starring in the next sequel to a major film franchise before your stomach acids touch semen. However, no amount of knotted cherry stems can save you from a slow season at the office.

It had been established before Christmas that Tripper would be taking a week long in-house tutoring course in new software, but by the time it came it felt more like a safety net. He may not get forty billable hours, but he would at least have something more to put on his timesheet than "GIS Folder Maintenance".

The topic of the training course was a shiny new 3D modeling software that you could use to program a small camera to fly around a digital environment like a paper airplane. As best as Tripper could see it, that's about all the software was useful for. He had spent days getting ahead of the instructor by following along in the manuals he, Kevin and the company IT specialist, Penn Zimmermann, had been given. Penn had spent most of the sessions asleep. Kevin tore out as far ahead of the instructor as possible until he hit a snag, at which point he would rock back and forth and knead his hands until he got his question answered one way or another.

The nation was now twelve days into new management. Tripper knew this because he had heard Penn ponder the thought out loud earlier in the day during lunch. A comment that on its face should not have been considered explosive, but given the current social weather it was equivalent to announcing to the room that you had a bomb before pulling a gun on a small child. Because of the differing of opinions between the employees of LMJ, lunches had been split into unofficial halves. The first half hour of lunch was reserved for the rebel scum, who sat in the downstairs meeting room and gossiped like 18th century colonial revolutionaries. Nothing of real substance came out of their hushed conversations. The second half hour of lunch was for the vocal minority of loyalists to the current national management. Nothing of real substance came out of their conversations either, but they were the exact opposite of hushed.

Tripper had no real interest in government politics. Entertainment politics, however, were another matter. He often drowned out conversations concerning bills, acts, vetoes and policies with a mental recitation of the upcoming films he had to see, who directed them and the filmmakers previous five movies. However, the films that had been receiving the most buzz were directed by filmmakers with at most two titles to their name. Times, they were a-changin' and not just in the White House. The previous summer saw the release of two films that, in Tripper's perception, received far too much attention, all do to entertainment politics. One was a remake of one of his favorite films, with what the media lovingly referred to as "a gender swapped cast." The main marketing campaign for the film was the overall understanding that if you didn't see it, or worse didn't like it, then you were a misogynist. Tripper wasn't a misogynist; he just knew it was going to be shit. Another film achieved veritable blockbuster status due to people whining on the internet that the scores and ratings for the movie were low and people needed to support it because it was, "really good and people need to stop being mean." Or something to that effect. These were the things that got Tripper riled up. But today, he was more interested in events that occurred much closer to home.

At around 8:15 that morning, Tripper was sitting next to Penn and rocking back in his chair as the instructor performed his daily task of finding the missing remote for the overhead projector. Penn gave the instructor a tired look before rubbing his eyes then pulling out his phone. Kevin watched with almost child-like glee as the instructor puttered from one end of the room to the other like a windup toy. It was during moments like this that Tripper thought of that scene from *Shogun Assassin*, when the Lone Wolf is in the tub with Cub and that other woman and he picks up his sword and closes his eyes, listening to the room as the camera slowly pans 360 degrees. Tripper knew that it would be a good eight minutes before the instructor was finally put together enough to start the class, so he seized the moment and closed his eyes.

The weather had been unseasonably warm since October, and today was no exception. Water that should have amounted to a decent snow fell sloppily from the sky in large greasy drops. Tripper listened as it splattered the sidewalk outside of the basement exit, almost a straight shot down the hall from the downstairs meeting room. After a few minutes, he heard a car door slam in the rear parking lot and heavy wet footsteps making their way up the sidewalk toward the door. Tripper opened his eyes and leaned over toward Penn to check the time on his phone. It was a little late in the morning for people to still be coming in. He slowly rocked back in his chair and turned his head to look out of the meeting room and down the hall toward the exit door. The footsteps got closer to the door, and then there was the overly loud metallic *crack* as the exit door lock was disengaged and echoed down the hall. The footsteps did not seem to be slowed by stepping through the door and Tripper made a mental note to be careful in the hall, because whoever it was didn't wipe their feet. He continued to balance his chair on its two back legs as he stared down the hall expectantly, waiting to see who had come in, but the footsteps never made it to the doorway of the meeting room. Instead they took the first right and walked down the hall past the main line of office-like cubes on the lower floor. Tripper furrowed his brow and raised one eyebrow as he craned his neck to follow the sound of the footsteps. They walked deep into the lower floor of the office before turning left, walking the length of the hallway and turning left again. By now, Tripper should have been able to see who they were, but the second door into the meeting room, the one that led into that hall, was closed. The soggy footsteps walked straight toward the meeting room before turning right and with great conviction marching into the basement file storage room.

Tripper squinted and turned his head so that he was side-eyeing the wall directly in front of him. The wall that the meeting room shared with the basement file storage room. After a moment he turned toward Penn and whispered.

"Who was that?"

"Who was who?" Penn looked up from his phone with a sleepy expression.

"Did you just hear someone walk into the office?"

"No? Why?"

"They went straight into the storage room."

"And?"

"Who's gonna come in through the back door and walk straight into the storage room?"

Penn shook his head and shrugged. He looked even more bored by Tripper's observance than he was by the one-man clown parade at the front of the room.

"I don't know. It was probably Clark. His office is right there."

Tripper gave a look of pained confusion, "Maybe."

Despite Penn's dismissal of the event, Tripper aimed his ears toward the room on the other side of the wall and listened intently. After a few minutes, he heard the sloppy wet footsteps emerge from the storage room and reverse course down the same path they had entered the building. Tripper looked from the open doorway, to the instructor who was now finally ready to start the class. The footsteps drew nearer the exit door and Tripper hesitated for a moment before standing and walking toward the door.

"Mayhew," called out the instructor, "is there a problem?"

Tripper froze in his tracks upon hearing his last name called out. It instantly took him straight back to high school even though he hadn't even seen the building in almost seven years. He leaned his head around the corner to get a better view down the hall.

"No, I just...," responded Tripper, "I thought I heard something."

Kevin laughed and turned towards Tripper, "You hearing things again, Tripper? Is the scratching in the walls this time or is it still in the floor?" He turned back toward the instructor and laughed, giving the instructor a second-hand chuckle.

Reluctantly, Tripper turned around and walked back toward his chair. As he sat down he heard the exit door echo down the hallway. Penn watched Tripper sit down and glanced at his phone before locking the screen and setting it on the table.

"Sales for copies of 1984 have gone up," said Penn sarcastically.

"A little late for that, isn't it?" responded Tripper as he settled into his seat, unable to pull his mind away from the wet footprints in the hallway.

* * *

Tripper stayed late that day. Later than he would have preferred. Georgie Boylen and a couple of the downstairs guys tended to stay a little late. Georgie the latest of them all. Tripper supposed that he was trying to avoid his home life for some reason or another. Georgie Boylen always reminded Tripper of a guy he sat next to during the summer of 2013 when he worked at Crystal Communications. He never caught his name, but Tripper was just as fine not knowing. The guy was Gary Rader, pre-police investigation. He never bathed, shaved, or combed his hair. He wore the same clothes every day. He looked like the love child of Steve Jobs and Bob Wozniak but just as old. On his desk was every prototype developed by Apple and IBM between 1976 and 1983 and all the paperwork to accompany it. At any point during the day, Tripper would be terrified by the sound of a submarine dive alarm and a voice screaming, 'Warning! Warning! It's *the wife*!' that was the man's ringtone. The man would sigh and take his time before answering the phone to carry out suspicious whispered conversations. Tripper enjoyed his summer stationed in what was known as "Siberia" in the far most northern wing of Crystal Communications, but he didn't enjoy that guy. He didn't enjoy Georgie Boylen either.

It was 7:30 before Georgie left. Due to the lull in work, Tripper had not been cleared for any over time, so he spent three hours hiding out in a downstairs bathroom reading *Zodiac Unmasked* and slowly draining his phone battery. When he heard Georgie close his car door and drive off, that's when Tripper made his move.

The basement of LMJ was dark and empty. The usual sounds of typing, coughing and the whirring of computer fans were gone. Tripper's footsteps seemed unnaturally loud for how softly he was walking. The bathroom that he had chosen to hide out in was three feet away from the door that the mysterious footsteps came through earlier that morning.

The rain still slapped and dripped outside. Tripper turned on his phone flashlight and examined the floor to see if there were any footprints from the mystery visitor. If there were any, they were lost and buried underneath the salty, muddy footprints of everyone else who went in and out of that door in the last eleven hours. Two trails led from the door and down the hall before they split into two directions; one leading in the direction he had heard the footsteps and the other leading to the meeting room. Tripper took the former.

The lights in the basement file storage room were off. Tripper's hand hovered over the switch for a moment before he dropped it. If he turned on the lights, someone would come back to the office. If he didn't, they wouldn't. He panned his phone's light beam around the storage room. Metal shelving units lined both walls and ran down the center of the long corridor. Boxes, loose papers, CDs, VHS, file folders, folded drawings, rolled drawings on vellum and paper all spilled off the shelves blocking the aisles between the stacks. Tripper looked down at the floor and back at the entrance to the storage room, illuminating the faded muddy footprints of the morning's phantom intruder. He followed the trail down the length of the cluttered corridor and around the turn to the very back of the storage room. The footprints stopped at several spots along the way and then start again. Whoever came back here knew what they were looking for; they just didn't know where to find it.

Water ran through PVC pipe into a hole in floor with an annoying persistent splash. Tripper finally reached end of the line. The footprints moved in a weird pattern before reversing course and trampling back over themselves. They stopped at an empty spot on the floor, then over to a shelf of dusty boxes before returning to the same spot, then leaving. Tripper kneeled down and held his beam level with the floor. In the light he could see a dusty outline roughly in the shape of a large rectangle. There had been a box there. There wasn't a box there anymore.

He stepped over to the shelf full of boxes. Maybe whoever came in put the box back up on the shelf? This was a theory that Tripper quickly dismissed. Why would you break into a disheveled storage room and then straighten up? Whoever found the box, walked out with it. On a shelf about chest high, a box caught his eye. On the front of the box, written carefully in black marker were the words **Shady Acres**. It sounded suspicious enough. Tripper lifted the lid and looked inside.

He had no idea whether there was something missing from the box or if what was inside of it should have been there at all. A stack of random papers was at the very top of the box. Tripper moved those aside to reveal two rows of bright orange, hardbound, field survey notebooks running the length of the box divided in the center by a thin piece of cardboard. The box jostled as he sorted through it and he noticed that on the right side of the stack of books flopped back and forth, whereas on the other side they remained tight against one another. One of the books was missing.

Tripper took note of the numbers written on the spines of the books in the incomplete row. Based on the sequence, the number was 594-02-1026. He picked up a couple of the other books and flipped through them. There wasn't really anything of interest, because there wasn't anything in them. They were all empty. Tripper closed the box and stepped away from the shelf. He turned off his flashlight and took a few pictures of the room before he left.

CHAPTER THREE

Californian Hills

Winter had passed, spring had come, and the year was rapidly closing in on summer and there was still no work at LMJ. Project managers' allusions to work on the horizon became a bad joke that no one thought was funny anymore. Except for Kevin.

The office was perpetually stiflingly hot, do to Robards' and Manovich's insistence that at seventy-seven degrees the office was cold enough to hang meat in. This was a phenomenon that Tripper had slowly learned was frustratingly common at every office he had worked in. There was always somebody, or a couple of somebody's, who bitched that the air conditioning was actually a refrigeration unit ripped out of an industrial sized restaurant freezer and would in turn crank the heat as counter balance. The building that housed the offices of LMJ Engineering was little more than a box made of un-insulated concrete block. It was a scientific impossibility for it to get cold between the months of March and September. Also, the near perpetual rainfall that summer kept the humidity bobbing some-where in the high eighty to low ninety percent range. Often times, the office would be muggy and overly hot while rain came down in buckets outside. Severe thunderstorm watches became somewhat of a weekly occurrence. None of this did anything to relieve tensions in the office.

In an effort to distract himself from the heating and cooling wars and busy himself during the lull in work, Tripper began filling his downtime by writing and doing research for a script based on the Best Picture Oscar scandal that occurred earlier that year titled *And the Oscar Goes Too....* The official story was that the envelopes had been switched. Tripper and many other people suspected a conspiracy. However, Tripper, in his typical fashion, took it *way* past the realms of believability and started connecting it to the death of Stonewall Jackson and the invention of the Slinky. He was also convinced that it had something to do with the Hollywood sign being changed to read 'Hollyweed' on New Year's Day. Everything including the title needed some work and he had time to kill. But all the while, at the back of his mind, he never stopped thinking about the alleged missing field notebook in the basement.

He had done some digging on the company's servers for anything regarding Shady Acres and had come up empty. The project number 594 matched no projects on company record. After about a month of searching, Tripper gave up. There was no way of telling if those notebooks even related to a project that LMJ had bid on. Since President Pissdrinker had taken office, funding to municipal development nosedived. Clients backed out of agreements with LMJ with increasing regularity. No one had money for infrastructure development or maintenance. Every once in a while, they would get orders for emergency repairs on collapsed sewer lines which was almost always directly followed by the client backing out of their agreement. Any one of these now absentee clients could have had started a development called Shady Acres and cancelled it a long time ago. It could have also been documents that the company inherited when they brought on a new client back in the salad days or when they hired a new project manager. There was no telling. But why was there a box full of empty field notebooks labeled with a non-existent project number in the basement? And why would someone steal one of them?

"What do you know about Shady Acres?" Tripper asked Penn upon entering his cube. He often went to Penn in search of work, anything that could give him some billable hours and he usually entered his cube by asking a question completely unrelated to why he came in the first place. Penn had grown used to this and indulged Tripper to avoid his own work.

"Shady Acres?" Penn said hunched over his desk staring at his monitors. "Like Green Acres? The Hundred Acre Wood?"

"Yeah, what can you tell me about the bad side of Hundred Acre Wood?"

"It's a bad scene. I heard the donkey has that kangaroo on the stroll."

"Rough gig," Tripper paused for a moment, so he could re-address his original topic. "But really, do you know anything about it?"

Penn continued to stare at his screen, but he wasn't really engaged in what he was looking at. It had just become reflex to always look busy. "Shady Acres? I know nothing. Why?"

"I had to scan in a bunch of drawings this morning and I hadn't heard of the project. I couldn't even find a project number for it. I figured it was something that was gonna be coming down the pike here pretty soon."

Penn finally pulled himself away from the monitor, spun his swivel chair toward Tripper and leaned back in it. He picked up his portable coffee mug and flipped it open but didn't drink from it. "My honest opinion, it's a conspiracy. It is the culmination of a more than fifty-year plan that is finally coming to a close."

Tripper stepped more inside of Penn's cube and half leaned on shelf. "It's a facility being built to house the props used to fake the Moon landing?" This was a game that Tripper and Penn played often. They didn't believe in conspiracy theories, but it was something that they took great delight in making fun of, seeing who could concoct the most absurd, yet believable, conspiracy theory on the spot.

"The Kennedy assassination, actually," Penn said casually. "They are building a full-scale replica of Dealey Plaza and they're naming it Shady Acres to throw off the scent."

"Not very covert."

"Neither was the Kennedy assassination."

"There was one that I read about just recently; that the death of Alex McCandless was actually a ploy by the fast food industry to boost sales. And the whole McCandless family was paid off to keep quiet."

"Who's Alex McCandless?"

"That Into the Wild guy. Wandered off *into the wild* of Alaska and starved to death. Sean Penn made a movie about it."

"Oh, like Christopher Knight?"

"From the Brady Bunch?"

"No, he was up in Maine or somewhere in there. He disappeared like thirty years ago and nobody knew where he went. Apparently, he moved into some abandoned cabin in the middle of the woods and would steal stuff from people's houses. They said that he committed, like, over three hundred burglaries."

"Woah, I had not heard about that."

"You should look it up. It's pretty interesting," Penn set down his cup and spun back around to his monitors. "Lemme guess, you're looking for work?"

"You know me so well," Tripper said sarcastically, taking out his pen and picking up his notebook from where he set it down on Penn's desk.

"It's gonna be a slow summer," Penn said to himself.

"As opposed to the slam-bam winter and spring we just came out of?" Tripper said, not attempting to mask his sarcasm. Penn was the only person Tripper was any sort of natural with. The two met on an intellectual level and shared a very dry sense of humor. Penn felt the same about Tripper; he just didn't care as much.

"Naw, they just hired a new intern for the summer," Penn said in his bored way.

"Jesus Christ." Tripper dropped his head and rubbed the bridge of his nose with his forefinger and thumb.

"Some girl," Penn didn't acknowledge Tripper's reaction. "I think her name is Montana."

"Great. How many of the partners did she blow? Or did they just find out the owner of the resume had tits and hired her sight-unseen?"

"I don't know," Penn shrugged lazily. "As long as I don't have to teach her how to use AutoCAD, I don't give a shit. I just got told about it this morning and now I have to start setting up her machine."

"When does she start?" Tripper asked. He wanted to have time to prepare for the coming of an interloper.

"Tomorrow."

"When did they hire her?"

"This morning."

"Sounds about right. That's the way they did it with me."

"She was abducted by clowns once." The words flowed as coolly out of Penn's mouth as if he just said what he was going to have for lunch. Most functions inside of Tripper temporarily ceased. He looked at Penn and shook his head sharply as he spoke.

"What?"

"Yeah. She was missing for like three or four months." Penn continued to look at his screen. He was now chatting with somebody and only half in his conversation with Tripper.

"She was kidnapped by clowns, man?"

"Yep."

"You're fucking with me."

Penn looked up from his monitor at Tripper with his sleepy expression. "No. Back, like 2013, 2014. She was walking from the parking garage down on the South Side on Carson when a white van pulls up and three guys dressed like clowns jump out, grab her, and throw her in."

"What the fuck?"

"It was online all over the place. It's why they started cracking down on all of those clown sightings on Staten Island."

"I thought that was all for the reboot of It."

"What?"

"The movie."

"What movie?"

"It! Stephen King's It. They're remaking *it*."

"Oh, no shit."

"No."

"Huh. I hadn't heard about it."

Penn looked from Tripper back at his screen. He was more looking through it than at anything it was displaying. He ran his tongue along his upper wisdom teeth with a loud squeak and a pop. After a moment of quiet contemplation, he began typing again. "Anyway, I don't have anything for you."

Tripper did his own distant pondering and stared down at the carpet inside Penn's cube. He had heard what Penn said, he just didn't care. "How did I not hear about this?"

Penn shrugged and then quickly typed something. "I don't know. It was all over the news. Go look it up."

Tripper turned around and left Penn's cube a changed man. He thought that the company had reached new lows when they hired that project manager off Craigslist. Now they were hiring Amy Smart via Barnum & Bailey as a summer intern. He returned to his desk and tossed his notebook near the outer edge, to make it look like he was busy, then sat down to investigate. It didn't take a very extensive internet search to turn up results.

Her name was Montana London, twenty-three as of 2014, a then recent graduate of Pitt University with a degree in mechanical engineering and, sure enough, she had been abducted by clowns. Tripper learned from an article on an online news source, *Graphite*, (not any local stations) that on June 9th, 2014 while walking from the parking garage at Station Square, a one Ms. Montana London was pulled off the street and thrown into an unmarked van by a group of three individuals dressed as clowns. They had a looped ten second clip of grainy black and white security camera footage that showed her walking down the sidewalk by herself, a van pull up, clowns bursting out of the van and then dragging her, screaming, into it before taking off again.

They had another video in the article, which was clearly shot before she was discovered, of an award ceremony that took place in March at the Soldiers and Sailors Museum just a few months prior to her abduction. She was receiving an award for achievements in mechanical engineering. The video had been trimmed down from a much longer video to focus only on highlights of her. She seemed like any of the other people Tripper had gone to school with, if not a little intense.

However, the weird thing was that there were no articles talking about her return. An internet search turned up a page of results for articles related to her disappearance, but not a one talked about her coming back. Maybe that's what the family wanted. It's bad enough their daughter was abducted by four guys in rainbow wigs and bag suits, the last thing they need is to kick the news anchor hornets' nest when they finally get her back. In any case, it was going to be a weird, slow summer.

* * *

The next morning, the small, predominantly male, office was a-buzz with energy. As the morning progressed, people became more and more excited about 'the new girl'. If it was just some guy showing up, there would have been a couple members of the office welcoming committee giddy with anticipation, but for the most part people could have cared less. It was guys with girlfriends and fully grown married men falling over themselves because the new intern had two of the same chromosome that left Tripper rolling his eyes.

The counter next to the fridge held a three-tiered stack of boxes from Dick's Donuts. Donuts in an office are about as noteworthy as sand on a beach, but the choice of Dick's Donuts gave Tripper another reason to groan. Dick's was a small local outfit that opened somewhere in the mid-fifties and had become a sort of staple in the area. However, in the mid-nineties, under the new management of the original owner's son, the pastry shop had taken a harsh turn from its classic mom and pop image with a change to its slogan. For nearly forty years, countless bags and boxes left the small-town donut shop with the words *"Dick's Donuts: That'll Do the Trick!"* emblazoned on them in chubby pink letters. Now for nearly twenty years, they bared the slogan *"Eat a Bag of Dick's!"* in the same pink font. Tripper toyed with the idea of sneezing on them before ultimately walking away.

At about eight o'clock that morning, when Tripper was about an hour into some podcast and researching the Macintosh half time commercial of 1984, one of the office secretaries, Alyssa Drake, swiftly cruised past his desk with a dark figure in tow. It was usually at this point in morning when new employees where being introduced that Tripper would make his leave for about ten minutes to avoid the always forced and awkward handshake. Instinctively, he started to get up, but he decided to ride this one out for a change. The likelihood that he would even share two words with this chick over the course of the summer was pretty slim, so he decided against leaving. He wanted to shake hands with and look in the eye of a person who was dragged screaming into an unmarked van by a group of clowns and lived to tell about it. "That's not the sort of thing that most people come out on the other side of," he thought to himself.

He could hear the rhythmic start and stop of footsteps come down the hallway behind him as she was introduced to the partners one by one. Carson Pembroke, the main head of LMJ's five headed Ghidorah, introduced himself in his usual over the top car salesman-like way. Tripper decided that he wasn't even going to stand up. Slowly they made their way to Kevin's desk directly behind him. Kevin sounded overly excited and rushed, but he was that way with everybody. Tripper faked opening and closing some PDFs as they reached his desk.

"And this is Tripper," Alyssa said in her affected, saccharine sweet tone.

Tripper turned around and reached out a firm handshake. He didn't look up to see who he was making contact with, until he felt his firm squeeze returned.

"Montana," said a cold direct voice.

Montana London was not what was considered to be attractive. Her body and facial features were in odd proportions to one another and while, as a whole, they made sense on her, they would have been considered outlandish and ridiculous on other people. Her dark hair was hopelessly un-maintainable and went in direct contrast with her pale completion, not in a way that reminded people of Snow White, but more of someone who had been bedridden for several years. The area around her eyes from her cheekbones to just under her brow was constantly dark and almost appeared bruised. Her ice blue eyes would dart at sounds or toward whoever was speaking and stare with an intensity that made even inanimate objects uncomfortable. The one thing that caught Tripper's attention, however, was her predominant canines. When she listened intently her mouth would open slightly, and her lip shape gave the illusion of a smirk that would reveal just the tips of her canines giving most people the impression that she was a vampire. This was not a perception she was ever proud of projecting, but one she had come to accept and would exploit if it benefited her to do so.

"She's our intern for the summer," Alyssa carried on.

"Nice to meet you," Tripper said with a cock of his head, as if what Alyssa said was interesting.

"Likewise," Montana said in the same cold direct tone.

"Tripper does mostly, what is it, GIS stuff," added Alyssa. "GPS maps, that sort of thing."

"Did you go to school for that?" Montana shot her eyes from Alyssa toward Tripper as she spoke. At this point, it was difficult to tell what was colder, her voice or her gaze.

"No, I learned it here, actually," Tripper replied in his own cold way. The difference in his delivery, as opposed to hers, was that he came across a little bit pissed. "I have a degree in mechanical engineering. They've taught me a lot."

Montana's eyes widened as she listened, and her mouth opened slightly exposing her predominant canines. When Tripper was finished talking, she slowly closed her mouth and set her jaw, sucking on her upper teeth with her bottom lip.

"Hmm," she said dismissively, her eyes looking through Tripper.

Tripper met her gaze and stared back up at her. Alyssa's eyes quickly darted back and forth between the two before finally touching Montana on the shoulder and leading her over to Robards' desk. When Montana finished her rounds in that section of the office and Alyssa took her downstairs, Tripper spun around and saw Kevin peering over his monitors at him.

"What was that all about?" Kevin asked both confused and excited.

Tripper shook his head and then spun back around to his own screens. "I don't have the first damn clue."

Somewhere around eight thirty, Alyssa dropped off Montana at the desk directly in front of Tripper. The cutting table directly abutted his desk making it a near constant thoroughfare for most of the office. And that's why they sat her across from him. They wanted a convenient excuse for random visits. The first person to do so was Hunter Musgrave. He came carrying a full box of donuts and a stack of paper towels. Montana quickly spun around in her chair at the sound of his approach, just in time for Hunter to set the box of donuts down on her desk.

"Hey, how's it goin'?" he said in his typical overly loud and disingenuously friendly way. He always talked like he had to address the entire population of the world while standing dead center in the crowd at Woodstock.

Montana showed no expression and looked from his hands to his face. "Hey," she said flatly.

"Hey, I'm Hunter. I'm a project engineer. I work downstairs. I didn't catch ya when they took you around. What's your name?" He spoke quickly and loud enough for the whole room to hear and then held out his hand to shake.

"Montana."

"Montana? Like the state, right?"

"Yeah."

"Cool, cool. Well, I brought these over I didn't know if you managed to get one before these guys, these...corn pones snatched 'em all."

"I can't do gluten."

"No, it's ok. Take a couple if you want to. We have a bunch. Do you like Dick's?"

Tripper rubbed his eyes.

"I have...a gluten...*sensitivity*," Montana said firmly. "I...*cannot*...*eat* them."

Hunter looked like he had all his batteries removed and his pull string clipped. It was a full four seconds before he spoke again. "Oh, you can't do gluten?" He looked down at the box of donuts as if to make sure what they were. "Aw, shit. I'm sorry." He continued to talk to Montana but looked around the room at everyone else as he spoke. "Here I'm trying to get you first pick and you can't do gluten. I'm sorry about that." Looking back at Montana, "You're probably gonna be allergic to just them sitting here, huh?"

"Probably," said Montana, her eyes wide and giving a sarcastic nod.

Hunter snatched up the box and held it away from her. "I'm sorry about that," he said doing his best to appear genuinely remorseful. "Can I get you something else? You want some cookies? I think we got some cookies downstairs."

"Do they have gluten?"

Someone clipped Hunter's pull string again. "I don't know."

"Probably not then."

"Aw, I'm so sorry." Hunter spun in a semi-circle addressing everyone else in the room. "You hear that, you greedy sonsabitches? The girl needs something without gluten. Miserable bastards," He turned back to address Montana, "I'm sorry about that. Next time we'll pick up some gluten free ones for you."

"It's really not an issue," Montana said quietly, drawing attention to how loud Hunter was talking.

Hunter tucked the box of donuts under one arm and held out his hand for another shake. "Well, if you need anything, I'm downstairs."

Montana gave the weakest handshake possible. "You said that already."

He was too busy riding his own roll to hear her. "I'll probably be sending you up some work at some point."

"Alright," she said with her sarcastic nod.

Hunter turned and walked away, once again addressing the whole room. "You guys got away this time. You miserable, greedy.... corn pones. Next time, pick up something for Montana, my new friend Montana, will ya? Jesus Christ." His voice trailed off as he went deeper into the office and then descended the stairs down to the basement.

That afternoon at lunchtime, Tripper watched Montana eat a homemade sandwich and a granola bar.

CHAPTER FOUR

Peace Frog

Tripper hated polo shirts, as he hated Hell, all Montagues and daily company lunches. Most of the employees and offices at TABLEU were nice enough, but everyone eating together at twelve o'clock sharp everyday was something that he just couldn't handle. He was able to get over the occasional visits from the office dogs and the flat screen tuned to the Game Show Network sooner than he was the lunches. He had just spent the last two years sequestering himself to dank, cobwebby college stairwells to eat alone. Now, during his internship, he was expected, daily, to join the entire company in the open kitchen at the center of the office for lunch.

TABLEAU Inc was a privately owned licensed CAD software distributor owned by Mark and Bernadette Powers. The Powers' were good people, in Tripper's estimation. A little bit on the hippie side, but Mark knew his stuff, pulled his weight and expected the same from his employees. This was something that Tripper admired and respected greatly. Bernadette managed the company finances and payroll. The couple shared a large office at the front of the building that was reminiscent of something you'd see in a movie about a newspaper outfit in the '40s. Their desks faced one another, like detectives, but were separated far enough to lay two dog beds between for their chocolate labs.

The rest of the offices ran the length of the wall and were made of, at times oddly shaped, wooden cubicles with sliding glass doors. Tripper's office was the approximate size and shape of a broom closet. When he stood up or sat down, his chair would hit the wall behind him forcing him to enter and exit his desk like a half-hearted racecar driver. The doors of all the offices looked out on the kitchen at the center of the building, so escaping lunch was an impossibility. The only people who didn't have offices in the wooden horse-shoe were the IT coordinator John Stanwicks and the off-site training specialist Noah Giuseppe who had neighboring offices in the basement, just down the hall from the training room, and the pantry for the catering company on the first floor.

Either lunch started early that day or work never really did. Tripper couldn't decide which. He sat on a stool at the bar in the kitchen looking up at the flat screen which was tuned to the news. Something Tripper would eventually come to understand would be a late motif in office life. The catering company downstairs had made their monthly delivery of out-of-date snacks and the rest of the employees were tearing open bags like they had spent a year on a desert island. Mark and Bernadette sat quietly in their office with the door closed. Tripper propped his head on one fist as he stared at the television, only half paying attention to Brant Reinhart's recitation of his favorite motocross riders.

"Where the hell was Batman last night, huh?" laughed Stanwicks with a mouthful of pork rinds. "Off bangin' Catwoman somewhere, probably."

"Jesus, Ann Half-a-bake?" replied Noah. "I wouldn't fuck her with a stolen dick."

"C'mon, man. Catsuit, tight leather, those fuckin' cat ears. Have you seen Love and Other Drugs?"

"Just because I blew you that one time doesn't make me gay, alright?"

Noah and Stanwicks burst into hysterical teary-eyed laughter, covering each other with half chewed off brand snack foods. Tripper strained to hear the television. Ten, possibly twelve fatalities. Some were children. The shooter was apprehended by the police just outside the theater. Tripper rubbed his eyes and wiped his mouth in disbelief. It wasn't for the reasons they were saying on the news. He didn't really know why.

"No. Fuckwads," Wes Cody waddled his way up to the table Noah and Stanwicks were sitting at. He dropped four bags of off brand nacho chips on the table and carefully did his best to sit in a rolling chair half his size, breathing heavily through his mouth. "Rooney. Mara."

Noah's eyes went wide, and his mouth curled into the shape of an O. He turned to Stanwicks who had stopped chewing and looked at Noah with the expression of a dead fish.

"You seen Girl with the Dragon Tattoo?" Wes suffered from the delusion that everything that he said was inarguably correct and his opinion, the only one that mattered. Tripper had had several fantasies of throwing him out in the middle of Oakmont Business Park Drive on delivery day.

Noah and Stanwicks hi-fived and laughed as if they caught each other looking at a Playboy. Wes sat back in his chair with a sickening creak. His greasy sausage sized fingers slipped and fumbled with one of the bags of chips as he looked at the two with his sleazy puppet master smile.

"I've gotten a lot of mileage out of her," he said with a grotesque amount of bravado. "Thank god DVDs can't get stretched out, if you know what I mean." He let out a contended fat man chuckle.

The laughing couple stared off a little bit sick at the idea of Wes Cody masturbating, but quickly smiled again as their thoughts returned to the original topic of conversation. Tripper turned around briefly to look at the trio, before shaking his head and turning back to the TV. In turning he bumped Brant's elbow knocking him out of the trance he had been put under while staring at a corn chip. He looked from the chip, to the bar, to Tripper before his attention was drawn to the newscast. He addressed the group behind him without turning around.

"Hey! You guys hear about the Batman shooting?"

"What, Batman shot somebody?" Stanwicks said with a smile sending Noah into red-faced hysterics.

"No," Brant continued matter-of-factly, "there was a shooting last night at a midnight showing of The Dark Knight Rises in Colorado." His eyes darted across the screen reading the scroll.

"Yeah, it sucks," Wes said not turning away from Noah and Stanwicks. "I wouldn't want to die in Colorado either." He gave his puppet master grin to Stanwicks and winked. Noah couldn't breathe.

"No," Brant said still reading the screen, "says this guy was calling himself the Joker."

"Bullshit," said Stanwicks, "It was probably some nigger pissed off that Black Panther hasn't gotten a movie yet."

Noah looked up at Stanwicks trying to catch his breath, "Black Panther," he said before descending into laughter again.

"Or Thundercats" Stanwicks added.

"No, that's the fudge packers like Thundercats," Wes added quickly. "They're supposed to be getting one here pretty soon anyway. The coons are still too pissed off about that wannabe thug in Florida to know about movies."

Tripper pressed his forehead into the heel of his hand and shut his eyes tightly.

* * *

That year had started off with a bang, on both a company and national level. During the twenty-four hours that the office had been empty on Christmas Day, a person or persons unknown had successfully hacked into all six of Crystal Communications main servers and made off with terabytes of information. In some cases, they didn't even bother copying files and just stole them all together. The interesting thing was most people at the company didn't even know that the files existed and when they finally learned about the hacking, they didn't really care. For weeks, parts of the country had been swept with a meteorological phenomenon that most people had never heard of before. It wasn't another round of what the President had so callously referred to as Snowmageddon; it was the first case of what laymen referred to as "intensely fucking cold". Pipes burst, power was lost, and schools and businesses were closed up and down the northeast; except for Crystal Communications.

Tripper sat at his desk late one evening, trying to catch up on work. Due to the weather he had come into work late three days that week and he needed to meet his AsBuilt quota if he wanted any chance of getting hired. He knew that he most likely wouldn't get in forty hours, but he could at least stay late and meet his quota.

He watched his breath crystallize as it left his mouth. Tiny glass-like shards of ice had built up inside of his nose. It was now eight o'clock at night and all the other employees had left, dropping the ambient temperature in the CAD office to freezing. His three coats weren't cutting it anymore, so he decided to take a walk to get the blood flowing.

Tripper picked up his *Teenage Mutant Ninja Turtles* mug and walked from his cube down the hall to the kitchen. The five coffee machines next to the fridge were empty, but the smell had permeated every hard and soft surface in the kitchen years ago. Tripper was not a coffee drinker, so this affected him not at all. He filled his mug with hot water from one of the coffee machines and dumped in two packets of hot coco mix.

He walked out of the kitchen, down the hall and into the lobby with a mug of hot liquid. Small acts of rebellion like this made Tripper feel more alive and in the vast, thankless, corporate machine and he felt that he should seize as many opportunities as he could. He stood in the middle of the rear lobby of Crystal Communications and examined the fake pine needles that were still on the floor despite the tree being taken down weeks ago. Looking up from the floor and at the ceiling four stories above him, he watched and listened as his breath crystallized with a sharp *crack* as it hit the air. It was easily ten degrees cooler in open four-story lobby than it was in the CAD room, and the temperature in his mouth had been raised by the hot coco. About fifty yards down a hallway to his right and behind two sets of security doors, Tripper heard all the refrigeration units in the café vending machines kick on at once. In the silence of the office building it sounded like someone dropping a car engine into an industrial sized metal mixing bowl. He didn't jump this time.

What did alarm Tripper was the gentle tapping coming from the glass exit doors behind him. He froze as the fight or flight instinct kicked in. Slowly he turned around and saw Melvin Cass, his CAD team leader, standing in the vestibule with a cigarette. It reminded Tripper of pictures he had seen of the glass smoking boxes in airports. Melvin motioned for Tripper to join him, then reached into his pocket and pulled out a lighter.

Tripper stepped into the vestibule and instantly wished he hadn't. Upon crossing the threshold, his legs immediately felt like refrigerated meat, his hands stung, and his nose began to run. He held the mug to his mouth and breathed into it for the steam before he took a drink.

"I'm sorry I interrupted you stepping outside to enjoy your tobacco refreshment, Mr. Cass," he said sarcastically. "I'll make this meeting brief."

"Fuck that," Melvin said, holding the cigarette between his lips as he lit it with one hand. "It's negative twelve. I'm not stepping out there for shit."

Melvin Cass was about six foot two, sturdy build with dark hair and beard that made him look not entirely unlike Wolfman Jack. And he was the only person Tripper got along with at Crystal Communications. They hit it off in his first week when, still without a machine and monitor, Tripper brought in a POP! of Michonne to put on his desk. He had felt overwhelmed being at a company so large after just leaving the small family run office where he had interned over the summer. Remembering the words of Derek Vineyard, he decided to throw up a flag; Melvin saw it. They bonded pretty quick, talking mostly about comics at first then quickly expanding to include movies and then it was all over. Tripper had been under a different team leader for the first year he had worked at Crystal Communications, unable to make any sort of connection. Finally, they relented and passed Tripper over to Melvin.

"The first twenty feet of this place smells like cigarettes anyway."

"They definitely need better ventilation," Melvin leaned his head back and blew a lungful of smoke at the ceiling. "What's got you here so late?"

"Quota," Tripper said, nonchalantly trying to avoid the smoke. "I've come in late this whole week. I'm not gonna be able to get in my hours, but I at least want to make quota."

"Don't worry about it. Most of upstairs has been called in sick since Monday. And with this whole hacking thing, nobody's gonna notice let alone blame you."

"That would make me feel a lot better if I wasn't a temp," Tripper did his best to not sound petty and looked away from Melvin as he took a drink.

"You've been keeping your numbers up," Melvin put the cigarette between his lips, stuffed his hands in his pockets and shifted from foot to foot. "Been keeping good hours. There's supposed to be something opening up here in the next couple of weeks. As long as you don't bring a gun to work or do a whole bunch of crack you should be fine."

Tripper let that hang there for a moment. He hoped that it would somehow make it stick in Melvin's head and make it come true. Melvin took a drag on his cigarette then reluctantly pulled his hand out of his pocket and took the cigarette out of his mouth. He looked down at the smoking tip, then out the glass doors and into the frozen desert landscape of the rear parking lot. Frost had entirely covered all the doors, but there was a circle about a foot in diameter that Melvin had scratched into one to look outside. Tripper looked down at the non-slip rubber mats on the floor encrusted with blue rock salt.

"Look," Melvin said, moving the elbow of his still pocketed arm to bump Tripper. He pointed to ghost-like words on the glass just below his porthole. "Jessie Eats It."

"Huh?" Tripper looked up and scanned the door.

Melvin pointed to the door with his cigarette hand, the smoke hanging in the cold humid air just above the tip. Tripper laughed and took another drink. His throat was starting to get hurt from the smoke.

"Who hell is Jessie?"

"That new girl in accounting. She's been going out with Ben since a little bit before Christmas."

"Jesus Christ, Ben Simpson?"

"No, Ben. Our Ben."

"That's not any better."

"Love is love, man."

"More like dumb meets ignorant," Tripper took another drink trying to keep a sore throat at bay. "What do you know about that hack, by the way?"

"Not much. My money's on Snowden."

"Good a guess as any. Did they ever fully explain what project the files were for?"

"Apparently, it's for wristbands for some theme park. Like security bands. Some sort of new technology their trying to work out."

"And they gave the project to us?" Tripper said incredulously.

"Supposed to be up and running sometime next year," Melvin said with a shrug.

"I didn't even know it existed."

Melvin raised one eyebrow and shrugged again, "We weren't supposed to." He blew out another lungful of smoke and looked at the tip of the cigarette, before looking back up at Tripper. "But fuck work. Have you been watching that True Detective?"

"I missed the first two episodes, but I caught up with it and watched the new episode on Sunday."

"It's fuckin' awesome right?" Melvin said with his big bearded grin.

"I had no expectations. I didn't even know what it was about, but two minutes in I was hooked. I'm shocked at how much I like it."

"Who knew McConaughey had it in him?"

"It sounds stupid, but have you ever seen Reign of Fire?"

* * *

It was hard to hear the TV over the people playing ping pong. The game had started somewhere around 7 o'clock that morning and had not stopped. It was now 11:45. The game featured a near constant change of players, but there was a core group of six that never left the table. Several members of the core group were responsible for introducing the smoker employees of Crystal Communications to the growing trend of vaping, which had become the preferred pastime between games, regardless of the fact that it was not allowed in the building.

The view of the parking lot outside the cafeteria windows was obscured by a row of hedges that employees would stand in front of and vape, sending obnoxiously large cherry, licorice, and maple scented clouds into the air. On days with more cloud cover, all the green of the hedges would sink into black and the vape clouds would look like exhaust emitting from smoke stacks, turning the hedgerow into a scale model of some 1940s German munitions factory.

Today was not one of those days, however. The sun shined relentlessly down on Water Haven Business Park, punishing anyone who dared to step outside for even a moment. Tripper had purchased a black plastic tray of iceberg lettuce and imitation chicken product from a vending machine and took a seat at a large round table in the middle of the empty room. He had covertly lifted the remote from a chair near the ping pong table when he entered the room and sat for a moment flipping through channels until he found *Jaws 2*.

A poorly gauged spike sent a ping pong ball rocketing across the room toward Tripper who instinctively covered his salad with both hands and ducked his head. The ping pong ball bounced off his head with a sharp *thwack* sending the corporate lotus eaters into a fit of theatrical, hysterical laughter. One of the players walked over, suppressing pretend chuckles as he held out his hand for the ball. Tripper picked up the ball and threw it at the guy's chest.

"Still haven't figured that garden hose trick out yet?"

"What?" he replied stupidly.

"Keep your balls to yourself, fuck up."

"Why are you being a dick? It was an accident."

"Yeah, your mother said the same thing."

"Asshole," the guy said as turned to walk away.

"Cocksucker," said Tripper under his breath as he looked back at the screen.

Tensions had been high at Crystal Communications that summer and Tripper was neither oblivious to it nor spared from it. The previous day, at that same hour, the lunchroom had been a madhouse. Where it was usually quiet and empty between the hours of eleven and noon, it was packed wall to wall with employees with lunchboxes and McDonald's bags and choked to death with vape clouds in a rainbow of flavors. Before Crystal Communications employees were free to eat at their desks during their lunch hour, they were now sequestered to the lunchroom for a weeklong exile after an incident involving Pepsi, vape oil and a stack of original drawings from 1998. As Tripper stood at the back of the room nursing a can of Coke, he surmised that most of the people in the room probably thought that they were going to beat the rush and eat early, changing the normally quiet lunchroom into the party scene from *Sixteen Candles*.

The television was tuned to the news, but the volume was off. A large percentage of employees were young business professionals with degrees in accounting, marketing and business management, so their knee jerk reaction to change the channel of any television in their presence to the news was nothing more than an attempt to keep up appearances. Tripper knew that the cafeteria televisions in the big fancy schools these assholes went to were tuned to the *Jersey Shore*, with the buttons smashed in and the remote missing, the same way it was at the two-year college he went to. He knew that if he changed the channel no one would notice, he just couldn't tell where in the detritus of lunches the remote was. Tripper took a drink of his Coke and looked out the window, over the hedgerows, and into the distance. Large white puffy clouds cruised leisurely over the hills, their mammoth shadows blackening out the sun to the cars and buildings below. He breathed deeply once, checked the time on his phone and turned back to the television.

Tripper's broadcast had been interrupted for a special news bulletin. Malaysia Airlines Flight 17 had exploded over Hrabove, scattering bodies and flaming debris across 19 square miles of eastern Ukraine. All passengers and crew were suspected to be dead. Cause of the accident: unknown. Someone had caught it on video. News footage showed people in paper suits walking through black twisted plane parts toward a blazing inferno in a green field under a grey sky. Tripper sipped his Coke and checked his phone again. As he glanced down, he saw the guy in the purple striped polo seated directly in front of him was also watching the television.

"How strange is it," thought Tripper "that in a room full of people in my age bracket only two people are looking at the television?"

He glanced up at the room. The junior accounting manager was picking at the pink jewels on her phone case and talking to the junior marketing manager who was checking her makeup in her phone's front facing camera. Across the room, two other CAD guys were staring at the girls, their faces smeared with red sauce, normally dead eyes glazed over with lust. The lotus eaters were blowing vape clouds like fog machines and attempting to clock a new company record for game length, all without breaking a sweat. Maybe it wasn't that strange.

Tripper looked back at the television, which was now displaying a blurry phone camera picture of one of his old high school classmates. The scroll at the bottom of the screen read: JASON TORMEN, 23, DEAD IN AUTOMOTIVE ACCIDENT. Tripper felt his grip slip a bit on his Coke. He hadn't seen Jason but once since he dropped out in tenth grade. Jason was a decent guy, not MENSA material, but he was ok on his own. It was when he was in large groups of people that he became a holy terror. Tripper remembered sitting across from him in eighth grade home-ec and talking to him about *Army of Darkness*. It was one of the very few times he ever really got to talk to him. After a while, a few other people joined the conversation and Jason wound up drawing a smiley face on his tongue with a black magic marker and running head first into a wall. The last time Tripper had seen him was the year after he had graduated. Jason was barefoot and shirtless, wearing only a pair of blue jeans dirtier than he was, running alongside a 98 Ford Ranger, pushing it down a hill trying to pop the clutch. Now he was on the news, dead.

Tripper pulled his gaze away from the TV and looked down at Purple Shirt in front of him. "I went to school with him," he said, trying to talk over the din of the lunchroom.

Purple Shirt spun around and looked up at Tripper. "Huh?" he asked, his eyebrows raised.

"I knew that guy," said Tripper. "I went to school with him."

"Oh, yeah?" said Purple Shirt, a little bit too interested.

"Yeah," Tripper said solemnly, more to himself than to Purple Shirt.

Purple Shirt turned around to face the TV. "No kiddin'." He slowly shook his head, taking a handful of chips out of a baggie and putting them in his mouth.

* * *

The wind felt like a bucket of razorblades. Tripper inched his way across the parking lot, along the driveway and down the sidewalk until he made it to the first set of stairs. It was a toss-up as to what he would slip on: the ice or the rock salt. He had made it the whole way up the hill to Niahm Labs without grabbing onto the railing; the journey back down was going to be a different story. As the pain slowly crept through the metal railing and into his bare hands, he silently cursed himself for leaving his gloves at his desk. He had procrastinated picking up the prototype for Harmon all day and, in the rush to get there before the lab closed, had left his gloves on the allen wrench set on his desk. At least his hands were dry.

Tripper walked into the empty, quarter-lit Design Engineers' office and dropped the prototype on Harmon's desk with a *crash*. The room filled with the sound of change falling as tools, hardware, pop tabs, and random metallic gee-gaws tumbled to the floor. He blew into his hands as he slowly made his way down the long hall back to his desk.

"If a prototype falls on your desk and only Tripper is around to hear it, does it make a sound?" he thought to himself.

He sat down in his swivel chair with all the grace of a frat house and put in his earbuds. Went he left for Niamh, he was in the middle of a podcast where three guys were bickering about the Guardians of Peace. Some obnoxious movie had been pulled from theaters before it was even released, all at the command of a foreign country. Tripper felt it was a bad move. So did the guys on the podcast. So did the President.

Tripper picked up a Phillips head off his desk cluttered with drawings and tools and spun around to the giant glass box behind him. He had no interest in working, especially with only ninety minutes left in the day, but he figured it was better than sitting on his hands and worrying about getting an air-strike for New Years. Many at Industrial Safety Engineers took the news regarding the Guardians of Peace as a joke, something that cluttered up their news feed. This was the case for most of the country as well. For other parts of the country, it was the Cuban Missile Crisis of the twenty-first century.

At quitting time, Tripper headed across town to Hanrahan's and got a booth to himself near the back. In his six weeks at ISE, Tripper had made a ritual of stopping at Hanrahan's every Friday afternoon. It was usually pretty slow around the time he got off work and the service was decent. It afforded him the opportunity to be out in the world and around people without the added effort of having to talk to anyone, save for the waitresses, who were fairly even keel.

The cooks in the kitchen argued hockey stats and put together the occasional plate while setting up their stations for the dinner rush. The bar back tried feebly to win back the heart of the head bartender who initially smiled at him and slowly waved the diamond on her ring finger, before eventually ignoring him altogether. After each visit to his table, Tripper's waitress would rush back to the soda fountain and type feverishly on her phone which she had hidden at the bottom of the napkin station. *Turning Tables* by Adele hummed through the nearly empty restaurant. Tripper read through a folder of papers he had printed out at work on the disappearance of Tara Calico as he took in the ambience.

The waitress returned to his table and set down a nearly over flowing glass of pop half an inch away from Tripper's papers. Tripper noticed the presence next to him before the glass hit wood. He looked up from the papers at the young disheveled waitress. Her appearance was that of someone who had just finished a lunch rush, but was still holding it together. She looked down at him with a smile and spoke with fleeting eye contact.

"I got you another pop," she said proudly.

Tripper looked at the three-quarters full glass he had been drinking from, to the overflowing glass whose puddle had overtaken one of his papers and was beginning to soak two others through capillary action. He raised both eyebrows before snatching up the papers and looking to the waitress. She continued to stare at him for a moment before her delayed reaction caught up with reality, forcing the smile from her face and a rag from her apron.

"I'm sorry about that," she said panicked.

"It's alright," Tripper said a little tired.

The waitress grabbed the cloth napkin from one of the other sets of silverware on Tripper's table and dumped the utensils out with a *clang*. Tripper separated the wet papers from his dry stack and set them both on the bench beside him.

"This girl, for some reason or another, has had a rough day," he thought to himself and kept his annoyance in check.

"Oh my gosh, I'm so sorry,"

"It's fine. Shit happens. Just don't do that with the soup and we'll be golden."

The waitress laughed nervously. She had somehow managed to soak herself from the stomach of her shirt up to her elbows. Her face, moments ago tacky with dried sweat, now glowed in the dim down light over the table. She brushed stray hairs from her face with one wet hand, while she held a pile of dripping rags in the other. Her proud smile had been replaced with an embarrassed smirk. She took a moment to breathe before holding out a wet hand to shake.

"I'm Cammy," she said red-faced, rolling her eyes.

"Yeah," Tripper said calmly returning the shake, "You said that earlier. But to be completely honest, I forgot."

She laughed nervously again, then stood staring. Tripper stared expectantly back at her. After a few uncomfortable seconds he began to slowly move side to side to see if her eyes would follow him. They did.

"Can I...*help* you?" he asked cautiously, still in motion.

Slow to react once again, Cammy's eyes widened, and she took a half step back touching her wet sticky hand to her mouth. "Oh my gosh, I'm so sorry. I was staring, wasn't I? Please don't tell my boss."

"If it's in regard to a skipped prescription, I may be forced to."

She laughed nervously again and turned her head away. "No, no, no. It's just...I...stare at people? and my boss says that makes people really uncomfortable and if I don't stop he'll fire me."

"Well, I'm not that interesting to look at, so I don't think you'll have that problem with me for very long."

"No, no, no. You're cool! I think you're cool! You come in here every Friday. I've seen you. Well not last week because I had to work Sunday and not Thanksgiving weekend because I took it off, but I see you all the time and I think you're cool."

Tripper tried to become very engaged in the paper wrapper from his straw. "Thank you very much, Cammy. It's nice to be appreciated."

"I'm so sorry I spilled pop all over your stuff. I just thought you needed another one."

Tripper stared at the table and lifted his three-quarters full glass, "Got one. Thanks."

"What were you reading about?" her eyes overly wide with excitement.

"Stuff," he said in the monotone delivery of his college and high school days.

"Was it Twin Peaks? I heard you talking about Twin Peaks once with Andy. That girl in the picture looked like Laurie Prescott. Did you know they are bringing it back?"

"That's what they say," Tripper picked up his coaster and slowly rolled it like a tire across the table between his thumb and forefinger.

Cammy bounced on her heels waiting for Tripper to say more. Finally, after a few moments when she realized he wasn't going to say anything else, she reminded him again, in her sugar fueled way, to call for her if he needed anything before taking off for the hostess station with her pile of wet napkins. Over the course of the meal, Tripper learned that she had been going to college for journalism but dropped out over the summer and that her parents named her after a character in Street Fighter. She showed him a tattoo on her right bicep of her namesake taken from a player select screen and a tattoo on inside of her right wrist of the Sega logo. Several times she let him know that he would be more than welcome to come over to the Christmas party she was having that weekend with friends. Tripper ate very little as he waited for his papers to dry out enough to put back in their folder, then paid his check at the bar and left. He didn't go back to Hanrahan's for a while.

* * *

The art of the company function, and specifically the company lunch, is difficult to master, but ultimately satisfying once the code is cracked. It had taken Tripper years to learn the right balance of being seen and being invisible. Also, in-house events were much easier to navigate and exploit than off-campus events. After years of service at several different companies, he was finally able to put his training to use.

Conversation and disingenuous laughter echoed from the cafeteria in the heart of ISE and down the artery-like hallways to the far corners of the building. However, Tripper was in a section of the building were sound could not penetrate and even less people could enter. He closed his pocket measuring tape like a lightsaber and muttered numbers to himself under his breath. The electric whine of the Sensor Room was constant enough to be ignored and loud enough to drive you insane. The sweet trickle at the back of his throat had started within seconds of entering the room and Tripper once again wondered how breathable the air was. He scribbled down a few numbers on his sketch and did a quick calculation in the corner of the notebook sheet. The glass casement for the epoxy paint shaker that he had been working on for months was half an inch too small. He was going to need a whole new order of 8020 and to explain, once more, to Harmon that the holes in the floor for the shaker needed to be re-drilled. He knew that it wasn't going to fit, but they drilled the holes before he even had the proper measurements. This was just another fuck-up, in a long line of fuck-ups that had been forced into his lap that he would have to take the blame for and deal with.

Tripper cursed under his breath and stood up. The Sensor Room was empty except for him. The leaking air compressor hissed and the automated soldering machine *cheep-cheep, whirr-whirred*. Tripper wiped his face with one hand and adjusted his oversized safety glasses before sliding his pen through the rings on the top of his notebook and making his way for the security code locked door with the air tight seal.

The distinct sound of Doc Marten's on linoleum echoed through the empty hallways as Tripper closed in on the cafeteria. The corridors of ISE overflowed with the sounds of conversation and Gene Wilder singing *Pure Imagination* which was equal parts a welcome comfort and an ominous warning of what lied ahead. Purple and gold balloons the size of three infants strapped together bobbed stupidly at the entrance. Matching streamers hung from the ceiling and swayed in the breeze of the crowd. A woman in a sad excuse for a Willy Wonka costume roller skated between people laughing maniacally as someone announced the presence of a chocolate fountain in a voice that was far too excited to be acceptable coming from an adult. Tripper knew the score. It was just as he had expected, only worse. He cruised past the first garage door sized entrance to the cafeteria and edged along the second. He spotted a tray of graham crackers and a wet cooler on the floor. Without slowing down he grabbed a stack of graham crackers before courteously bumping into someone and excusing himself as he pulled a dripping can of Coke out of the cooler, then booked it down the hallway toward Human Resources.

The Human Resources department was just as dead as the Sensor Room only without the whirring and the sweet tickle at the back of your throat. Tripper walked over to the coffee station, set the graham crackers down on a napkin and leaned against the counter. The flat screen over the garbage cans was, of course, tuned to the news. An unknown white male had just walked into a predominantly black church in South Carolina and shot nine people. Tripper cracked his Coke just as Alex Punn, the Mechanical Engineer in Tripper's Design Engineering department, strolled around the corner.

"Well your ass isn't on fire," he spoke without looking at Tripper, "so I don't know why you were running that fast."

"Crowd Induced Stress Syndrome," Tripper announced with a sigh, "Terrible affliction. Sweeping the eighteen to twenty-five demographic. I get my license for medical marijuana next week."

Alex stared at the television and leaned against the coffee station with both hands in his pockets. He nonchalantly pulled out his right hand and moved it toward Tripper's stack of graham crackers. Tripper cleaned up a small puddle of Coke with a napkin and slapped Alex's hand away without looking.

"Animaniacs?" Alex asked, staring at the helicopter footage on the television.

"Something like that," Tripper was trying to clean something sticky off the palm of his hand.

"I heard about this before the Oompa Loompa thing," Alex said with a mouthful of graham cracker. "Says he did it because of Freddie Gray."

"Where'd you hear that?" Tripper had finally gotten his hand clean. He slid the graham crackers away from Alex.

"Twitter."

"Figures. I heard about the Boston Marathon half an hour before it was announced on the news."

"There he is," Alex said pointing to the picture of Dylann Roof on the TV. "He kinda looks like my cousin."

"Better call home," Tripper took a drink.

"Nah, screw it." Alex finished chewing the graham cracker and brushed off his hands over the garbage. "I'm busy."

CHAPTER FIVE

What's He Building?

The rain came down hard and steady. The grey clouds swirled and blew from west to east with no end in sight. Work was at an all-time low and the partners were out of town on business. Tripper called in sick, but he didn't take the day off.

Tripper had been doing some research into Shady Acres. After some extensive digging online, he had turned up an article from 1983 covering a ground-breaking ceremony for a new housing development. The developers and the architecture firm went bankrupt before the project was complete. All the big wigs dropped off the map soon after. A back trace of the property developers and real estate owners yielded two addresses in Imperial off Route 30. Current deed holders: unlisted. The story sounded just as suspicious as the name, but it was more than he had to go on than previously.

A trip to the thrift store over the weekend had been kind to Tripper. He came out with well-worn Carhart jacket and a shirt for a water company in Manhasset, New York. As long as anyone he happened to encounter didn't read the logo on the breast pocket too closely, he would be in good shape. However, considering the weather, it didn't seem likely he would have any reason to take his jacket off.

A little after eight in the morning Tripper passed the houses on the hill overlooking Route 30 then circled back and parked across the street. They looked more ominous now. Normally, they just appeared empty. On brighter days you could see through the closed curtains clear out the windows on the other side. Their lawns manicured by persons unknown but always maintained. Their sheer curtains obscured the normally breezy, lonely interiors. In the rain, they held secrets. The grey light of the overcast sky prowled and crept through the empty houses like wide eyed seething animals; guarding something that they felt no one had the right to see.

Tripper sat in his car staring at the steering wheel and clenching his fist. Something inside of him was afraid. He knew what he was doing, but he wasn't entirely sure why. He had been lied to and used by every company he had worked for, but somehow this was different. Those in the know were far too aggressively tight lipped. The mystery surrounding Shady Acres was notably more cryptic than other company secrets Tripper had been aware of. Usually companies hid embezzlement, money laundering, preferential employee treatment, inferior manufacturing processes, contract fraud and the sexual escapades of their golden boys. Shady Acres did not fit the bill. Tripper wanted to know why. He wanted to know who he was working for.

He grabbed his prop clipboard and real notebook and ran out into the rain. He was soaked before he crossed the road. Tripper ran to the eastern split-level ranch first. Once he got there he wished he hadn't, because there was no porch. He stood under what little eave there was and used his hands to block out the light as he tried to peer inside. Rain poured down the window and the back of Tripper's shirt, making it impossible to see. He stepped back from the window and walked over to the sliding glass door. He thought to himself that it was a lost cause. Already soaked to the bone, he decided to at least give it a shot before packing it in and going home to fight pneumonia. With no more effort than it took to open his office door at TABLEAU, the sliding glass door at the first Shady Acres mystery house slid open.

Inside it smelled like new carpet and something strange. The sound of the rain slapping onto the concrete patio in front of the door echoed through the house like an empty cardboard box. Tripper hesitated a moment before stepping inside and shutting the door behind him. It was unnervingly quiet, except for the rain. There was no furniture. Just the open floor plan reminiscent to many mid-century split-level ranches he had been in before. He stood at the bottom right corner of the rectangular living room. In the opposite corner of the room was the entrance to a hallway that led to the rest of the house.

The carpet had been recently vacuumed, but there were several sets of footprints that led from his spot near the door to the hallway. Tripper wiped the rain off his face with his free hand than quickly made his way across the carpet, trying his best to not drip. When he made it to the mouth of the hallway he heard high pitched electronic beeping. The rhythm was constant, and it sounded like it was coming from somewhere deeper in the house.

Tripper transitioned from the carpeted living room to the faux hardwood flooring in the hallway. He followed the beeping down the unlit corridor to the first room on his left. What should have been a bedroom had been adapted into a rather high dollar server room. A large desk sat in the far corner from the door holding up three 22-inch monitors and a large triangular computer with throbbing multicolored lights. Once Tripper stepped into the doorway, he recognized that the sound was an uncharged back up battery for the tower. The shrillness of the beeping bounced off the walls and stabbed into Tripper's ears. He walked over to the set up and, with his index finger covered by his jacket sleeve, pressed the power button on the shrieking back up battery. It took him a moment to recover from the sound. The beeping reverberated in his ears for longer than he cared to think about.

A scuffling sound moved through the small room. Tripper froze and panned around the room with his eyes. Nothing appeared to be moving, but the sound persisted. There was tininess to the sound, like a recording played over low quality speakers. Tripper's eyes scanned across the computer screens and stopped when they saw movement. Each screen was broken up into four quadrants, all displaying separate video feeds. Several of the images were blue, but the rest showed several different rooms from security camera angles. He leaned in toward one that looked strangely familiar and realized that it was filming the door he had used to enter the house.

On a separate monitor, the image was moving. The camera recording the image had fallen over and was displaying the image almost upside down. Tripper turned his head to reorient himself. It looked like a high-class hotel suite. There was an open window in the background that blew out the picture. The autofocus shifted in and out several times before focusing on the buildings outside. It looked like the skyline of the Las Vegas strip. A chill shot up and down Tripper's spine.

He took out his phone and had managed to get a few pictures of the set up before he heard the front sliding glass door open. Instinctively, he stepped back from the computer desk and slammed into the closet doors behind him. Several sets of footsteps accompanied by loud voices entered the house and moved through the living room toward the hallway. Tripper fumbled with the closet door handles before stepping inside and softly closing them behind him.

"Jesus Fucking Christ, it's raining like a son of a bitch out there," said the first male voice. "Why didn't we bring umbrellas?"

"Because you left them in your wife's car," said the second.

"Look, now the carpet's gonna get soaked."

"It's fine."

There was in unmistakable sound of muffled screams. The sound of shuffling footsteps followed by the sliding glass door closing.

"You want me to take him downstairs?" asked a third voice.

"Yes," said the second.

The footsteps began to make their way toward the hallway. Tripper pressed himself into the corner of the closet and watched the floor through the louvers of the closet door. The footsteps went down the hallway past the bedroom before walking down a set of stairs somewhere deeper in the house.

"And I wore my fuckin'... nice shoes for this, too. Why didn't somebody tell me that today was the day the Jolly Green Giant was gonna decide to take a piss and I would have worn fuckin' rain slickers or some shit."

The sound of shoes scraping and shuffling on a dirty finished concrete floor echoed from the basement. There was a loud thud followed muffled screams of pain. Tripper pulled out his phone and began recording a video. He opened the closet door slightly to pick up the sound better.

"How are you feeling, Bellini?" said the second voice, distracted.

The muffled voice let out a long scream then began to cry. A metallic scraping sound followed by a noise reminiscent of a shower curtain hook. There was the sharp cracking sound of three quick slaps.

"Don't give me that," the second voice continued. "You got yourself into this situation, forcing us to get you out of it. *We're* doing all the work."

"There's a lot worse ways to go out, Ben," said the first, "but for a lot better reasons."

The muffled screams grew more intense before they were silenced by a wet thud.

"Shut up," said the first voice. "Shut up. I don't want to hear it anymore." The voice became deeper and more sinister, "I like giving people second chances, Bellini, but I like my money more."

Upstairs in the closet, Tripper's jaw dropped. He recognized the phrase and because of that, he recognized the voice. It was Carson

Pembroke. That meant the first voice was most likely Bart Gerlicher, the second biggest head of the LMJ Ghidorah. He couldn't put a face to the third voice.

"Open it up," said Pembroke.

There was a shuffling of feet, then a deafening silence. The house filled with the sound of the hammering rain. It tapped against the glass with hurricane insistence. Bellini let out a low muffled cry around his gag.

"*Jes*us," said Gerlicher, "he's fucking puking."

"Good," said Pembroke, distracted. "Let him choke."

Tripper stood in the bedroom closet holding his phone out through a crack in the door. Aside from occasional shuffling footsteps, no sounds came from the basement for a few minutes. Then finally Pembroke spoke.

"Is he done?"

"Yeah," said the third voice. "He's done now."

"Good," exclaimed Gerlicher, clapping his hands, "'cause I'm fuckin' starving."

"Call Kowalski," said Pembroke, "tell him to come by here later tonight and clean this place up."

"Pa-stra-mi! Pa-strami," chanted Gerlicher.

"Make sure he has everything packed up and ready for the barbecue. Let me know if he needs anything."

"Yes, sir," said the third voice.

"Pa-stra-mi! Pa-stra-mi!"

"Yeah, yeah. We'll get your pastrami. You're buying, though."

The three men started walking up the stairs.

"Me?" said Gerlicher laughing, "Why the hell am I buying? You're the one that makes a hundred twenty-five a year!"

"Because you forgot the umbrellas, that's why."

"Aww, c'mon!" laughed Gerlicher.

Tripper pulled his arm into the closet as he heard the men approach. A whiff of cigar smoke blew into the bedroom and the heavy footsteps moved to the carpet and out the sliding glass door, leaving the sound of the rain to take over. Tripper was alone in a house with a dead man.

CHAPTER SIX

Body Reprise

Tripper waited a few minutes to be sure that they had left. Finally, he crept out of the closet and into the bedroom, illuminated by the light from the monitors. Everything sounded much louder than before; the rain, his footsteps, the creaks in the floor. He slowly stepped out into the hallway, the smell of cigar smoke hung thick in the air. Using the trail of wet shoe prints on the floor he was able to trace back to the door that led to the basement. He turned back toward the living room. The grey light coming through the windows cast no shadows. He was truly alone.

Standing at the top of the basement stairs Tripper wished he had brought a weapon. He didn't own a gun, nor did he have any interest in owning one, but what did he need a gun for? The only thing alive in the house was him. And the invisible animals that guarded it. He reached into his pocket and pulled out a pen. After years in the office he learned that it was bad luck to go anywhere without a pen, because they had more uses than writing. The devices that a pen could be modified into were seemingly limited only by one's imagination. He clicked his pen open then made his way down the stairs.

The staircase seemed oddly familiar. He had hit the first landing before he had figured it out. It was just like the stairs at work that led down to the basement. Shady Acres and the LMJ office building must have been built by the same company. The treads creaked with each step. The dirty finished concrete floor opened up below him as he descended. The floor was covered in dirt, like peanut shells in a Texas themed restaurant. It looked clean. Not like potting soil, but high-quality dirt that was nothing but the dirt itself; no twigs, rocks or dead insects. He looked around when he reached the bottom and saw it standing upright in the corner.

"So, this is what they are doing when they are out of town on business," thought Tripper.

A dark-haired man in his mid-thirties was strapped to a wooden St. Andrew's cross. His face was purple. Duct tape covered his mouth and vomit leaked out at a loose area near the corner. His eyes were half shut and rolled in the back of his head. A tube ran out of his arm and was connected to a bag on an IV stand next to him. The switch dial controlling the flow of the drip had been closed, but fluid remained in the line. Rain pounded on the roof and against the basement window.

There was a metal tray on a stand a few feet away from the man. It held a few surgical tools, a small vial and a hypodermic needle. Tripper leaned down to read the vial without picking it up. The label read: CAFFEINE AND SODIUM BENSOATE INJECTION, USP 250 mg/Ml – 2mL SINGLE DOSE VIAL FOR IM OR SLOW IV USE. Tripper pulled out his phone and took a picture.

He noticed a familiar hum buzzing under the sound of the pouring rain. Upon turning around he saw a large vending machine standing like a sentinel on the opposite side of the room. It too looked like something from the offices of LMJ, from a distance. The top three rows were bags of chips. Below that, the standard pretzels, cookies and snack cakes moving down into candy bars and small bags Skittles. The third row from the bottom contained travel sized bottles of lube in various brands, scents and flavors. Below that were condoms, then the very bottom row were small "discreet" sex toys and different drugs wrapped in small clear plastic packages. Not professionally packaged, but with care.

There was an old portable hospital cabinet on wheels pressed up against the far wall. Tripper tucked his hand inside of his jacket sleeve and pushed the door open with one finger. The cabinet was full of gauze, alcohol, tourniquets, hypodermic needles and hundreds of small glass vials, their labels ranging from CAFFIENE AND SODIUM BENSOATE, to DELAUDED, to FENTANYL, and MORPHINE. After a quick mental calculation, Tripper decided there were enough drugs in the cart to get him and his entire bloodline incarcerated for most of the next decade. He snapped a few pictures of the cart, the vending machine and the corpse on the cross before heading upstairs, out of house and into his car, leaving behind Shady Acres for good.

CHAPTER SEVEN

No Splash

Tripper took the weekend off. He battled his way through the continuing rain and weekend tunnel traffic and caught himself a day pass to the Carnegie Museum of Art and Natural History. The thoughts and ideas swirling through his head gave him no peace. He wanted to fill his head with the thoughts and ideas of people greater than he was. Or at least of people who existed in a time before housing plans and intravenous drugs.

Times were slow during the summer at the museums, torrential downpour or not. Tripper was thankful he hadn't stumbled onto the Shady Acres mystery in September or he felt he would have gotten no peace whatsoever. He strolled his way through the plain white halls lined with priceless works of art and was reminded of *Vertigo* and by default *Dressed to Kill*. Neither of them were favorite movies of his and, granted they both involved murder, they gave him something else to crowd his brain with and he was thankful for it.

He sat on a bench for a while and worshipped at the altar of Van Gogh. It was one of his more obscure paintings, but Tripper was still thankful to be sitting face to paint with the maestro, at least for a while. The mountains and valleys of dried pigment. Considered 'impressionist' only by the intoxicated and people who couldn't process more than one thought at a time. He knelt down on the ground, knees pressed hard against the wall and looked straight up at the painting, giving himself a sort of profile view. A passing security guard didn't take too kindly to Tripper's form of appreciation and requested that he either stand or return to the bench. After some time, Tripper gave Vince a silent nod of appreciation and continued through the museum.

Tripper walked slowly and noiselessly as possible through the great empty halls. His scuffed and water stained Doc Marten's clopped against the marble floors like an amputated horse. Somewhere in the back of his head the radio had kicked on *The Maestro* and he found himself humming along to it, but he didn't know for how long he had been doing it. After a while he wandered into a giant hall full of stone sculptures. He looked around the large empty space and furrowed his brow. He had been to the museum many times before, but the area now looked oddly familiar. His brain flipped through files and Rolodexes so fast he couldn't tell if the sound was echoing through the room or not. After what couldn't have been more than a few seconds it clicked.

"This is where they shot Flashdance," he thought.

Several aspects of this realization confused him simultaneously. *Why*, in all the years he had been coming here had he not realized this before? *Why*, did he not put two and two together when he saw the film years ago? *Whose* bright idea was it to imply that dance tryouts are held in an art museum? *Where* is Montana going so fast?

Tripper snapped back into reality watching Montana London very quickly and purposefully walk along the upstairs balcony carrying a black leather folder and a manila envelope. She did not notice him below her and rounded a corner, putting her on the section of the balcony directly above him. Tripper quickly stepped out from underneath of the balcony, his footsteps echoing clumsily through the room, breaking any sense of being covert he might have had. She was gone. Tripper ran out of the Hall of Sculpture to the Grand Staircase and climbed it to the second floor. He mentally retraced her path as he climbed the stairs and ran straight for The Heinz Architectural Center seconds after he reached the top.

He stumbled into the Architectural Center to find no one inside. His overly loud footsteps echoed through the room and Tripper once again became aware that he was in a museum and did his best to straighten himself out, while simultaneously looking for a glimpse of Montana. He wasn't sure why he was following her, but he knew it would pay off if he found her. There had to be a reason more than coincidence that two employees of LMJ would be at the Carnegie Museum of Art and Natural History on the same weekend during a storm. Tripper knew why he was there; Montana was the one who was suspect.

He quickly walked the length of the room toward the doors that led to the Heinz Galleries. Tripper stepped into the center of the hall and calmly looked both ways, standing on his toes to see over the displays. Near the end of the hall to his right, he saw a Montana shaped figure standing near a bronze statue of a samurai. Tripper made a bee line for her, doing his best to look nonchalant. When he got about ten feet away he turned and faked looking at a post-modern cubist painting of pears and raspberries. He wasn't sure what to say and quickly searched the painting for answer. Finally, he turned toward her and feigned surprise.

"Montana?"

Montana snapped her head up from the description plaque for the statue. "Tripper?" she said with equal but more honest surprise.

Tripper made his way over to her and held out his hand to shake. His mind shot back to the Christmas party scene in *Eyes Wide Shut* and he did his best to imitate it. "Hey, what brings you here?"

"Art," she said sarcastically, raising both eyebrows and tightening her mouth.

"Well, that makes sense," he said with a laugh.

"What brings you here?"

"Same. When things get busy at work I pretty much live here, y'know? Try to clear my head."

"It hasn't been busy at work," she said with a slight shake of her head. Her words echoed through the hallway of the museum and then died. It was a little lie, but Tripper had been caught and he knew it.

"Well," he said after a long pause, "there's work and then there's *work* and sometimes one is more stressful than the other."

"I understand." Montana seemed less on edge. Her quips and barbs while still sharp, came more relaxed and conversational than

Tripper was used to. Tripper suspected it was due to not having five guys trying to jump her simultaneously. "What do you do for a hobby?"

Caught again. Tripper was not good at lying and while part of it seemed ridiculous, he couldn't tell her that he went to the museum to forget the terrible things he had seen after breaking and entering into a supposedly abandoned building. "Oh, just stupid little shit, y' know? It's mostly boring dumb stuff that makes people look at you weird."

"Really?" she said jutting out her chin quickly. "What did I drive to get here?"

Tripper shook his head in confusion, "Pardon?"

"Hmm," Montana bit her lip and the inside of her cheek at the same time.

"What did you...drive to get here? I have no clue."

"I know."

Tripper cocked one ear toward Montana waiting for her to speak again. She didn't. She just stared into him with her cold blue eyes and chewed on her lip with one fang, searching Tripper for answers to questions he didn't even know she had asked. A man with a goatee and dressed all in black walked up behind Montana and then stood in between her and Tripper. He looked from Tripper to Montana, who didn't acknowledge him but knew he was there.

"He's ready to see you now, Ms. London."

"'K," Montana said in her cold, flat manner.

"Who?" asked Tripper, still confused.

"The ghost of Andrew Carnegie," Montana said sarcastically, raising her eyebrow and tilting her head to one side. "I have a date to talk to him about boring dumb stuff that makes people look at you weird."

Tripper felt like he had been slapped in the face with the entire Wholy Fish Market, but he didn't know why. Montana chewed her lip at Tripper and took two steps back before turning and following the man dressed in black out of the hall. Tripper watched the two go through the exit door at the back of the room, dropping it with a loud metallic *clang* that echoed off every surface in the room. Once the sound dissipated, Tripper paid another visit to Vince.

* * *

Tripper spent maybe another hour at the museum before taking his life in his own hands and heading across town to the South Side. A man had been shot and killed outside of a bar on Carson Street back in May. It had been the most recent event in a string of violent shootings and assaults that had occurred over the last several years. Tripper had been good to stay away from that side of town, but there was a sandwich shop there he liked, and he didn't suppose that there would be much of a chance of getting shot in broad daylight in a sandwich shop during a rain storm. Thankfully, the shop wasn't part of a chain and he had no intentions of robbing the place.

Tripper sat in the back of the restaurant his back in a corner, facing the window, drinking Coke over ice out of a wax paper cup. The restaurant was small and mercifully empty. The Crosley Suitcase that was once faux black leather was now covered in stickers for local bands and sat on a stool behind the counter spinning *When We Were Young* by Adele over the jerry rigged sound system. The roller derby coach behind the counter wore a purple bandana around his head and sliced tomatoes with his back to the dining area. The only other diners in the shop sat at a two-person table near the window by the door. The cosplayer porn star girlfriend sat facing her hipster brewmeister boyfriend across the table and texted three other guys. The hipster brewmeister boyfriend sat shoeless, the back of his brown flannel shirt pressed against the condensing widow as he drank Jagermeifter from a hipflask and sexted with his girlfriend's best friend. Tripper was in the eye of what had, up until the last four years or so, been both the dream and reality of his generation. It was strange to think of how fast fads had changed. Things now sat in a nether region between fads and most people seemed to be in a holding pattern until they were told what to do next. Nothing that was going on around him was really out of fashion yet. But it had been around long enough that it was no longer considered fresh and quirky but run of the mill. Like the cosplayers thumbs as they hovered over the keyboard of her phone, everything was in stasis. Ready to jump on the next thing once they found out what it was.

All of this made Tripper very tired. There was nothing profound to learn from all of this, despite what journalists and the media told him. Every motion his generation had made for the last seven years had been watched and analyzed like a new subhuman species. Buying habits, spending habits, favored forms of communication, where they were going next and why they were going there. At first, he had bristled at the way he and his generation at large were being written and spoken about. Given the horrendously unoriginal and unflattering moniker of millenials: selfish, narcissistic, triggered, liberal and gender fluid. Tripper didn't identify with any of these traits (he believed himself to be liberal until the definition of the word changed to mean that you automatically took a stance of righteous indignation on all issues, and opposed any and all opinions that could be considered mean or rude, despite the reasoning behind them, at which point he stopped associating himself with the word) and, in the beginning, battled that the media was wrong and just making broad generalizations about a generation that they did not, and could not, understand. Then eventually, he just gave up. There are only so many Comicons he could attend and Mumford and Sons albums he could be accosted by in movie theaters before he gave in. The media was right. The millenials were losers. But he didn't have to fit the archetype.

The derby coach behind the counter made sure that his hands were clean enough for an operating room before flipping the record. The brewmeister boyfriend sighed at his phone and twiddled his hair between his fingers. The cosplayer girlfriend gave him a smile with her straw between her teeth and itched the Sandshrew tattoo on top of her right thigh. Tripper wished he had brought a book. It had taken him over a month to chew through *Hitchcock Truffaut* and he now just wanted to be done with it so he could move onto something else. His mind quickly flashed on a vision of himself sitting in *that* shop amongst *those* people reading *that* book. He took one more drink of Coke before throwing his trash in the can by the counter and stepping outside into the muggy afternoon.

Steamed rolled up off the sidewalk in the hazy city sun. Tripper looked east down Carson Street then headed west. He walked past the Barsotti Building toward the tattoo parlors, gyro shops, dojos, pizzerias, bars, psychic shops, comic book stores, cash for gold joints and vape shops into the heart of East Carson Street. He took a mental note when he passed Diesel (known to the rest of the world as Mawby's Bar) that he had hit two *Flashdance* locations in one day without even trying. He checked the traffic and jaywalked across the street to read the boards outside of the Rex Theater to see who was coming. He had missed The Orwells in May, but the Melvins were going to be there at the end of July and Dick Dale was coming in mid-August. A poster for some band he had never heard of listed dates for a national tour including a show in Billings, Montana.

Montana hadn't been this much of an issue in Tripper's life since third grade. Capital: Helena. He stepped back from the bills and burped some of the more colorful ingredients that were on his sandwich. A young girl in a Rugrats shirt and denim shorts covered in tiny blue stars walked passed him and sneered. Tripper shook his head and mumbled under his breath.

"Fuck you, you don't even remember the nineties."

He looked further down the street to the west. From where he was at, there was about a mile and half more to go before the spot where Montana was abducted. Tripper pulled out his phone and checked the weather. It was due to rain in about a half hour. He would never make it there and back in time. A grey wall of clouds was already beginning to make its way toward the city. He pocketed his phone and turned back in the direction of his car.

Traffic was starting to pick up on his way back to his car. Several rain drops were splattered across the windshield. Tripper started his car and turned around, weaving his way through pedestrians on his way back to East Carson. It took a minute for traffic to clear up enough to allow him onto the road. The warm yellow light that had flooded the streets mere minutes ago was gone. It was replaced by lead grey clouds and the occasional flash of lightning. The rain was slow in coming.

Tripper watched a homeless man pull a pair of bolt cutters out from underneath his coat and steal a bike near the Shephard Fairey piece outside of the Beeehive. It was the right time of day for it. The weekend warriors and the hardcore alcoholics were starting to stream into the strip, upsetting the balance quickly and sharply enough that no one would realize what happened until it was too late. Tripper was thankful all he saw was a bike theft.

He passed under the T and slowed down as much as he could as he approached the Station Square parking garage. The rain was just starting to stop messing around and get serious, but he still rolled down the passenger's side window for an unobstructed view. The stoplight stretched across both west bound lanes like the arm of a giant statue of Death at some seasonal haunted house. Tripper approached it with a corresponding amount of trepidation. He looked down the exit lane from Station Square and could see the security camera, but the lane itself was too crowded to see the actual location of the crime. People walked across the entrance and exit lanes, most of their bodies obscured by cars leaving nothing to be seen but floating disembodied heads. For the first time, Tripper thought of how strange it would be for one person walking to be the only thing on that road. His mind flashed back to the grainy black and white video. She didn't seem happy about the whole affair, but she didn't seem to fight too hard. More like she was startled then fighting for her life. And why clowns? And why did she just reappear? And why was she at the museum earlier? Tripper's weekend off wasn't going too well.

CHAPTER EIGHT

Macombs Dam Bridge

Tripper had had enough of the world and went home. The sandwich he got earlier didn't agree with him, so he decided to forget to eat again. At ten o'clock he turned on Adult Swim and forgot about that too. The mixture of cool blue twilight and warm sodium street light leaked in through his venetians and cast the shadow of an absurd jail cell door across his framed *Full Metal Jacket* poster. Everything inside of his apartment felt jumpy and paranoid, but it was better than the oppressive menace of the rest of the world. Tripper usually had delayed reactions about things and the weight of the past week was finally landing on him.

He muted the television and dropped *Psychedelic Jungle* on the turntable. He wanted to take a sonic scrub brush to the room and make it livable again. Shady Acres. Drugs. Bodies in the basement. Montana. Why was everyone acting so cagey? Well, LMJ made sense. Nothing that they were involved in was anything you'd really want anyone to know about. Montana must have known about it too.

Adult Swim wasn't pairing well with The Cramps so Tripper switched it to *LA 92*. Made about as much sense as Fruit Loops and turpentine but he hoped the pairing would distract him. He had never asked Montana about Shady Acres, but he never thought to, either. She was too new. But it would make sense. Work gets slow, so they hire a new employee? The lull in work is a result of Federal cuts to municipal funding. Why is she so suspicious of everything? She's hiding something. Why was there a book stolen from the basement for a project that everyone denies exists? That one is still shaky. Clearly the person who took it didn't want anyone to know it was stolen, but why only take one book and not the whole box? What is the significance of the number 594-02-1026? May '94? The company was established in August '79. The number pattern was different than other project numbers. The sequencing was off. Too many for a phone number. *Voodoo Idol*.

Tripper jumped on the computer. The lights from the television screen flashed and flickered through the room with a high pitched electronic whine. Lux, Ivy, Kid and Nick buzzed and boomed over the static pop of the turntable. Tripper looked up police call signs. 549: MALICIOUS MISCHIEF. 1026: CLEAR. It was sadistic and humorous in equal measure. Tripper decided that it was probably the desired effect. 02? It must have just noted that it was the second house. He stared through the monitor wondering what the numbers were for the other house. And furthermore, what was in its basement.

Who was Ben Bellini? Benjamin Bellini. Benjamin Bellini LMJ. Benjamin LMJ Engineers. Benjamin Bellini Pittsburgh. Nothing. What was Pembroke talking about with money? And there was something about a barbecue, too. The company picnic wouldn't be until mid-July. It seemed a bit premature to start getting ready at the end of June.

Tripper's mind flashed on the vomit leaking out of the duct tape over Bellini's mouth. He stood up suddenly from his computer and began to pace the room. The humidity was condensing on the walls and dripping from the ceiling to the floor, leaving discolored streaks on the paint. Tripper felt like he was breathing water.

CHAPTER NINE

Southbound Pachyderm

It was coming up on forty years since they captured the .44 Cal-
iber Killer. Most of the people at LMJ were biting their nails with
excitement in anticipation of season two of *Stranger Things*.
Manovich was sitting with his feet propped up on his desk watching
Rick and Morty full screen. Two years running now, he had been
chewed out during his review for having YouTube pulled up while
he was working. This was his childish form of protest. Tripper sat
at his desk reading *Son of Sam* by Lawrence Klausner. He bit down
hard on the clicker of his pen as he felt the sweat run down his back.
Every window on his side of the office was closed.

It was about an hour till lunch and Montana still hadn't come
in yet. Kevin said that she had called in sick, but Tripper called bullshit. She was her regular smart-ass, shifty-eyed self on Saturday. Unless she ate some bad shrimp or released monkeys from an animal
testing facility on Sunday, she was faking it. Tripper knew it, but he
also knew no one else gave a shit. Except for Hunter who had cruised
her desk twice an hour since he came in.

Tripper felt sick. Not in a faker, Montana London sort of way, but it did have to do with her. He had become increasingly disgusted by the likes of Hunter Musgrave, who would not let her be, and Georgie Boylen, who took overtly sadistic delight in piling multiple projects on her in a week and waiting for her to squirm. She did a couple of times, but Boylen was so close to her desk, Tripper thought he was standing on her shoe.

It was Monday. The following day was the Fourth of July. Most people had taken the day off. Those who came in that day showed very little interest in doing any real work and made no efforts to mask it. Tripper, still hopped up on weekend paranoia, filled both of his screens with work and read his book as if it were some sort of manual. This was more pretense than the current audience was worth, but he didn't want to get sloppy.

The bells on the front door chimed as someone left for an early lunch. The heat was stifling and somewhere between desert and swamp. Carson Pembroke all but padlocked the thermometer to prevent anyone from dropping the temperature below 80. The air smelled like stale dust, hot printer and barbecue potato chips. Tripper stepped outside to get some air.

The brush growing at the base of the reinforcing wall for the expressway swayed and bounced in the wind. The leaves turned over exposing their white underbelly. Tripper noted that it was going to rain. He faced away from the sun and looked up. The sky was clear cellophane blue. When the rain hits, he thought, it's gonna be fast and hard. He pulled out his phone and checked the time. In five hours, he would be free and clear of this place for twenty-four breezy summer hours. He wondered, if the rain continued through to the next day, how long it would take people to figure out that you can't keep matches lit in the rain. He took in a deep breath before heading back into the hot box.

The basement side door slammed behind him and echoed down the ramp into the seminar room. Every time Tripper had used that door since January all he could think about was that day. When the sloshing footsteps walked in unannounced, marched through the office, then reversed course and left. He would revisit the storage room every once in a while, just to check. Nothing ever changed. Rather than go past the vending machines and back upstairs to the office, he hooked a right at the end of the hallway at Boylen's cube and followed the path of the mystery footsteps to the storage room.

The light was on, which Tripper thought was strange. With the office all but deserted, he couldn't think who would be down there. After taking a few steps, he could hear shuffling and rustling deeper in the room. He tucked his book under his arm and slowly crept around the boxes and chairs toward the angle of the storage room. Whoever was in there couldn't hear him. He pressed himself up against a wooden set of drawing storage drawers and cautiously leaned around the corner. About halfway down the length of the room stood a person dressed entirely in black, complete with leather gloves, flipping through a box of folders. Their clothing was pristine, as if it had never even touched air before. However, the strangest thing was the person's full-sized mascot head of a sinister looking bald eagle. The eyes of the eagle glared at each file with the low simmering intensity of a homicide detective. Tripper couldn't move. After a moment the human hands attached to the eagle head stopped. The head snapped in Tripper's direction. The eagle's right hand reached under the left side of its jacket and pulled out a Glock Model 19 and leveled it at Tripper. There was a loud bang.

Tripper opened his eyes to see that he was still standing. The gun toting anthropomorphic eagle was still standing too. It stood, motionless, aiming the gun at Tripper. There was a scream upstairs, the sound of running footsteps, another bang and thud that made the entire floor above them shake. In a flash, the eagle took off running straight at Tripper. He moved to the side as far as he could in the tight walkway. The eagle slammed into Tripper with its right shoulder and knocked him off balance, sending him to the ground. He watched as the figure disappeared around the corner and ran out of the storage room.

The loud bangs and thuds continued above him. There were slow heavy footsteps that preceded each bang. Tripper became aware of his heavy breathing when he began tasting dust. He had pressed himself so hard into the floor he had almost become part of it. He reached into his pocket and pulled out his phone. His phone was locked up. Whoever was upstairs was using a cell phone jammer. There was a second set of footsteps that approached the first.

Then there was nothing. The silence seemed to last an eternity. Tripper listened closely but no doors opened or shut. He slowly lifted himself off the ground to his knees. He crept with assassin stealth toward the door. The office was unnaturally quiet and strangely alien. Nothing really looked the same.

Tripper stepped out of the storage room and into the hallway. It felt like it had been hours since he was last there, but it couldn't have been more than a few minutes. Quickly and soundlessly he moved down the hallway and through the back door of the seminar room. He made his way to the door that looked down the hall leading to the steel exit door he had walked through what now must have been days earlier. The footsteps on the floor above him began to walk toward the stairs that lead down to the basement.

Tripper booked it down the hallway, like Barry Allen on amphetamines, and slammed into the door creating the loudest noise it could possibly make. He cursed as he stumbled to the ground outside of the office and skinned the palms of his hands on the cement sidewalk. An explosion like a small bomb went off over his head and the door that had not fully closed slammed into his ribs and knocked him off balance. A sickening metallic chime rang through the door as broken glass sailed down on him.

"I've been shot," Tripper said aloud as he climbed to his feet and took off running through the rear parking lot toward the neighboring office building. "I've been shot. I'm bleeding to death. I'm gonna die. Two small children and a dog are going to find my body in the washout behind this building."

Another incredibly loud explosion went off behind him when he hit the side parking lot. It was followed by a shower of glass and a sound like gravel hitting aluminum.

"I'm dead. I'm pumping all the blood out of my body as I run. The buckshot has severed several major arteries and I'm leaving a trail of blood like the Mississippi River."

Tripper cleared the neighboring office building and crested the small hill that led down to a hardware store parking lot. He did his best to run down the hill, but wound up falling and sliding most of the way. The sound of his shoes against the pavement slapped and echoed in the manmade ditch where the hardware store stood.

He ripped open the door and jumped from the pavement to the tile without touching the sidewalk.

The hardware store was large and mostly empty at a little after ten in the morning. Tripper was forced to take shelter there once years before when a rainstorm hydroplaned his car into the parking lot. The employees were less than friendly or understanding and he never forgot it.

Tripper ran over to a check-out lane and ripped the phone off the counter. The clerk at the adjacent check-out lane took a few moments to process the event and stood up with all the intensity of a stoned koala.

"Hey. What are you doing?"

Tripper searched the cradle of the cheap plastic office phone for instructions on how to call out of the store. "How do you call the cops?"

"How do you what?"

"THE FUCKING *FUZZ*, NIMROD! HOW DO I CALL OUT?"

"Nine then the number," the clerk stared wide-eyed at Tripper, his hands held in the air just slightly above the level of the counter.

Tripper punched in the numbers and waited for the dial tone. He could hear his heartbeat in the earpiece. He wiped the sweat off his face and felt the sting as he rubbed it into the wound on his hand. Suddenly, he became aware that *Somebody That I Used To Know* was droning over the radio. It sounded even worse now than it had in the past.

"911, what's your emergency?"

"There's been a shooting at LMJ Engineers on South Hampton."

"Ok. What's your name?"

"Tripper Mayhew."

"Ok, Mr. Mayhew, anyone been shot, sir?"

"I don't know. I was shot at. I heard the shots."

"Are you injured?"

Tripper looked down at his shirt and pants. He was sweating profusely, but seemed otherwise unharmed. He stepped out from behind the counter to be in full view for the other clerk.

"Am I bleeding?"

"Who?"

"ME, FUCKNUT! AM I FUCKING BLEEDING?"

"No?"

Tripper moved his mouth back toward the mouthpiece. "I think I'm ok."

"How many shooters are there?"

"Two. At least that's all I heard."

"Are they in the building now?"

"I don't know. I ran out, I'm down the street at a hardware store."

Hunter Musgrave ran into the store breathing heavy with eyes like a dying animal. His face, chest and hands were spattered with blood. He quickly scanned the room and then ran toward Tripper. "Mayhew! Mayhew, are you alright?"

"Hold on a second," Tripper said into the phone. "Jesus Christ, are you bleeding?"

"They fuckin' shot Pembroke, man." Hunter's voice didn't really sound different than its usual public-address level of intensity, but his eyes were jacked wide open. "I was in his office with him and some guy in a Obama mask with a shotgun just walked in and fuckin' shot him. His head is all over the god damn room."

"Yeah," Tripper said into the mouthpiece. "No, there's a co-worker here with me. No. He's covered in blood, but he's not shot. Our boss. Says he was in the room when it happened. A male in a Barack Obama mask with a shotgun."

"There was another one in a Biden mask, too."

"There's a second shooter with a Joe Biden mask, he says."

"I saw them get into a car and drive off, that's when I chased after you."

Red and blue lights flashed through the windows. Tripper looked past Hunter's shoulder at the police cruiser as an officer stepped out of the car and walked toward the door.

"Yeah, they're here now. Thank you."

The jar-headed officer strolled confident but cautious toward Tripper and Hunter with his hand on his sidearm. He locked eyes with Hunter. "You call about the shooting?"

"No, he did." Hunter said pointing at Tripper.

"Are either of you injured?"

"No," said Tripper, "that's our boss's blood."

"Alright," the officer looked around the store grinding his teeth. He stared at the clerk and motioned at the back of the store with his chin. "Is there anyone else in here?"

The clerk stared at the officer with the same stoned koala stare he gave Tripper.

"Sir!"

The clerk shook his head slightly as he snapped out of a daze. "Huh?"

"Is there *anyone else* on the *premises*?"

The clerk shook his head and pointed to Tripper and Hunter. "Naw, man. Just those two."

The officer kept his steely glare and turned back to Tripper and Hunter. He took his hand off his side arm and motioned with two fingers for them to come towards him. "Gentlemen. Come with me." The officer taxied Tripper and Hunter less than a block back over to the offices of LMJ Engineers. Hunter zoned out through the window and bobbed his knee like a Victorian textile machine. Tripper counted three police cruisers and two ambulances parked haphazard in the small parking lot.

"Was there anyone else in the office with you when the shooting started?" asked the officer as they stood outside of the flashing cruiser.

"Uh..." Hunter said looking toward the sky.

"There was me, Alex Manovich, Kevin Baird---"

"Pembroke."

"Carson Pembroke?"

"Yes. He's our boss."

"Gentlemen, I regret to inform you that Mr. Manovich, Mr. Baird and Mr. Pembroke are dead."

"Shit." Tripper dropped his head and rubbed his eyes.

"There are several other bodies inside that have yet to be I.D.'d. We are currently waiting on more buses to pick them up."

"There was another shooter."

"Pardon?" The officer furrowed his brow and hesitated as he slid his notebook into his back pocket.

"I was in the basement and there was another shooter with uh...in a eagle mask."

"An eagle mask?"

"Yeah, like a mascot head."

"Like the Nittany Lion?" The officer stared through Tripper as he took down notes with sharp quick strokes.

"Yeah, but an eagle. Like a really fucked up looking eagle. Sorry."

The officer looked down at his notebook. "Did the suspect shoot at you?"

"No. They pointed their gun at me, though. And they had a handgun. A pistol. Glock. I think."

"Why do say that?"

"I grew up around guns."

"Do you own any guns?"

"No. I just know about them. Kinda."

"So, you're sure it wasn't a shotgun?"

"No," Tripper felt sarcasm begin to rise in his voice. "It was definitely a handgun. Not a shotgun."

The officer jotted down a few more notes then slid the notepad into his back pocket. "Thank you, gentlemen, for your time. If you would, please, don't leave the premises until I or one of the other officers has dismissed you."

Tripper glanced down at the officer's name badge. Kowalski. His eyes shot back up to the officer's face and he did his best to hide his contempt and suspicion.

"Sure thing."

Over the course of the next several hours Tripper slowly made his way from the mass of people gathered outside and toward the shade near the back of the building. He eventually realized that he was still holding his book, but he didn't read it. The two ambulances already in the parking lot were loaded and driven away, three more taking their place. Five bodies altogether. Tripper didn't know who the other two were. Even though he had been there for almost three years he still didn't know everyone's vehicle. He knew enough that some people brought out their motorcycles and sports cars in warmer weather, but that was it.

So far, it looked like Tripper and Hunter were the only two that survived the LMJ Massacre. He looked around the parking lot for his fellow survivor, hoping that he wouldn't have to step out into July's vengeful laser sun to find him. After a quick scan of the area he found him. There on the outskirts of the parking lot, near the recycling dumpster stood Hunter Musgrave and Officer Kowalski. The two laughed and carried on like they were already living it up at some Fourth of July picnic. Aside from the black and blue and the striped polo spattered in blood, they were only two beer cans away from a cookout. Tripper had read about strange behavior exhibited by victims of traumatic events, but Hunter was pushing it. He didn't look like a guy who was all that tore up about being a mere shotgun pump away from death just hours earlier.

Officer Kowalski stood sideways to Hunter with his arms folded across his chest. Hunter screamed something that echoed across the parking lot. Kowalski's face curled into a sneer as he let out a hyena-like laugh and bent over at the waist. Hunter faced Officer Kowalski with his chest puffed out and his arms back and to the sides as he looked around addressing his ever present invisible audience. Tripper moved about ten feet closer and hid behind someone's obnoxious dinosaur of an SUV. He pulled out his phone and zoomed in tight as he began rolling video.

"You *know* what I mean, right?" laughed Hunter. "You *know* what I mean. That's not the kind of stuff we're into."

"What a fuckin' dumbass," said Officer Kowalski, trying to breathe.

"I know right? Like, I mean, like this isn't some sort of Shady Acres shit we're dealing with here *anymore*. We're onto bigger and better shit!"

"Is this gonna be your first time up there?"

"Dude, this is the first time they've *had* it up there. We're gonna get to break it in like some skeeze on prom night."

"When are you heading up?"

"Whenever the fuck you decide to let me leave, man!"

Kowalski laughed a looked over Hunter's head up toward the office. "They should be wrapping up pretty soon. I'll see if I can get them to move that bus and I'll let them let you out. There's no real reason to keep you around anymore."

"Coo'."

"Where's your buddy at?"

"He's probably off takin' a shit down by the creek or somethin'. HEY, MAYHEW!"

Tripper almost dropped his phone. He shuffled for a minute as he tried to stop recording. He cracked his neck to one side to straighten himself out then held the phone to his ear. With all the nonchalance of Wooderson, he stepped out from behind the SUV and looked up toward Hunter and Officer Kowalski. He kept his book pinned underneath his arm and held up one finger to help sell the illusion.

"I'm gonna have the EMT's move their bus so we can let you out!" said Kowalski. "Where's your vehicle?"

Tripper took his book out from underneath his arm and used his hand to point up the hill toward his car.

"Alright. We're gonna get you out of here."

Tripper nodded and began walking toward Hunter and Kowalski. Hunter held out his hand to Officer Kowalski and patted him on the shoulder.

"See you at Fallingwater, man," he said low.

Kowalski gave him a sly smile, "See you there."

CHAPTER TEN

Sneakin' Out the Hospital

The storm hit during his ride back home. As he drove down the hill from Robinson Township toward the Moon exit, Tripper watched the sky change from a soft cool grey to a near black charcoal grey on a razor thin line. The air pressure increased, and his ears popped as he approached the black leviathan of clouds. He watched sheets of rain pour from the sky turning the dusty grey road to the dark slick color of pure oil. Tripper rolled down the windows and cupped the air in his hand as he drove, feeling the ambient moisture build up and bead on his skin. The first few sprinkles hit the windshield about two hundred yards from the storm. A bright flash of light glowed through the thick blackness above him and a *crack* of supernatural proportions echoed down the expressway. He quickly rolled up his windows as the frog sized drops of rain smacked against the windshield. The intensity of the storm was on a level that no other storm that summer would reach.

Tripper backed into his driveway just as the last few rain drops fell clumsily onto his car. He had never been to Fallingwater, so he didn't know how long it would take get there. After a quick wardrobe change (and pouring a little bit of alcohol on his hands) he was right back out the door. According to some navigation app he was about two hours away from Fallingwater. Not including traffic and construction.

Tripper turned on Creedence's *The Concert* and took off for Bear Run Nature Reserve. He made it back across the Allegheny County line, all the way up to the Fort Pitt Tunnel with very little fanfare. It was early enough in the day that he was going to miss rush hour and late enough that he missed the lunch parade. Things slowed to a crawl with construction when he got into the city. Tripper theorized a conspiracy made by the construction workers to intentionally back up traffic at random times of the day to increase the chances of accidents and receive workman's comp. It was a pretty cut and dry theory compared his exchanges with Penn.

"Oh shit," he said out loud to an empty car. "Is Penn dead?"

The thought hadn't occurred to him until now.

* * *

The rest of the ride was pretty quiet. Tripper would fight with the radio occasionally, trying to decide if he should listen to something and get out of his head or not. He didn't want to turn it into a road trip, but he didn't want to go into whatever he was going into depressed and paranoid.

Tripper reached the edge of Bear Run at about six thirty. The GPS said he was ten minutes away. He pulled over at a little farmer's market convenience store to get something to eat. A lifelong believer in the philosophy of working smarter not harder, he decided that it would be better to eat now than push his luck. It would also give him a chance to talk to locals and get in tune with the area, assuming they were open to conversation.

The bell on the door jingled over-enthusiastically as Tripper stepped in. The store was filled with the smell of stale bread and Pine-Sol. Wood paneling covered every wall in 8-inch-wide strips that ran from floor to ceiling. The butterscotch linoleum tile on the floor was old and worn, but well maintained. There were a few tiles here and there that had been replaced over the years leaving the occasional foot by foot square that was off shade from the rest of the floor. Wire shelving units covered in bags of chips, loaves of bread and bottles of motor oil stretched five deep to the drink coolers on the back wall. The Good Humor cooler near the counter purred like an old cat as *Love Will Turn You Around* played over some hidden radio. Tripper took a few cautious steps before he felt eyes on him.

"How's it goin'?" came a man's voice from somewhere near the back of the store.

"Not too bad. How about you?" Tripper said as a conversational reflex.

"Purdy good, purdy good." The man's accent was affected just for that response.

Tripper walked down one of the aisles taking his time to check out the shelves. The store was nearly identical to so many that he had grown up going to it was almost pointless to remark upon it. He grabbed a bag of sour dough pretzels and made his way to the drink coolers in the back. The man sighed and then made a sound like hands slapping denim covered knees before walking towards the counter. Tripper looked through the coolers until he found a bottle of Coke.

"Where you comin' from?" asked the man in a friendly but reserved way.

"Zeli," Tripper matching the man's tone.

"Where's 'at?"

Tripper finally looked over at the man who was now behind the counter. He was an older man, with white and grey hair combed back in a style from somewhere in the 1950s. He wore a buttoned down blue work shirt with the top two buttons unbuttoned. One arm leaned on the counter and with his hand pointed out towards the front in a shape as if he were holding a cigarette, but there wasn't one.

"Zelienople," Tripper lifted his head in the man's direction and walked over toward the counter. "Up near Evans City."

"Oh, that near Cranberry Township?" The old man leaned back from the counter and rubbed his knee with one hand.

"Yeah," Tripper gave the man a conversational grin.

"My daughter lives up around there."

"Oh, yeah?"

"Yeah, she works at ISE, building sensors."

"No kidding."

"Yeah, she been up there...bout fifteen years now."

"Wow." Tripper raised his eyebrows and pushed out his bottom lip as he nodded.

"Yeah, she likes it pretty good up there."

"ISE is supposed to be a pretty good outfit."

"As long as they treat her good I don't care how good of an outfit they are," the old man gave Tripper a big smile and flicked his thumb across the butt of the invisible cigarette. "I tell her all the time she went from buildin' sandwiches to buildin' sensors." He let out a low dry raspy laugh synonymous with lifelong smokers. Tripper moved slightly to the side to dodge his breath and covered it up by shifting his weight from one foot to another.

"You guys have sandwiches?"

The old man spun to his right and pointed to the large white deli case with one finger. "Got some right here. My wife and my daughter used to make 'em, then just my daughter 'n now just me. I'd make you one fresh, but the slicer's on the fritz." Tripper could tell by his voice that the old man was winding up to tell a lengthy story. Judging by how clean the store was, he probably didn't get to talk to people much.

"Whatcha got goin' on in here?" Tripper knelt down and stared into the case.

"I used to tell my wife all the time 'No one wants to eat a sandwich made by a man! Sandwiches always taste better when they're made by women!'"

"There is a certain level of truth to that." Tripper stroked his chin as he scanned the case and thought, "I'm sure women with culinary minded husbands would disagree."

"Then my wife passed away and it was just my daughter. And now she's up there in Cranberry and now nobody wants to buy sandwiches!" He let out his dry raspy laugh again.

"Well today's your lucky day. Can I get one of your turkey sandwiches, please?"

"Comin' right up," the old man did his best to hop off his stool then shuffled over to the deli case. "You headin' over to Jellystone? You sure you don't need a couple?" He laughed.

"Nah, if anyone gets jealous I'll just tell 'em to come over here and talk to my man...I didn't catch your name."

"Hank's the name. Hank if you want to be friendly, Henry if you're my mother." He stood up from behind the deli case and shuffled back over to the counter.

Tripper set the pop and pretzels down on the counter. "What's the damage?"

"$5.15 'll do it." Hank stared back at Tripper with surprisingly white teeth.

Tripper took out his wallet just as the doorbell let out another obnoxiously loud jingle. Hank gave the door a quick glace then used his forearm to wipe the counter.

"Aww, here comes trouble. Get outta here, we don't need your kind." Hank did his best to hide his smile as he spoke.

"You shut the hell up, Hank, or I'm liable to just not come back," the second man's voice talked to Hank with a friendly smile. "Tryin' to hurt my feelings."

"What's goin' on, Bud?"

Tripper laid the money on the counter and slid it toward Hank who picked it up and dropped it into the drawer without counting it. Tripper could live with being 85 cents short.

"Same shit, differ'nt glockenspiel." The man named Bud grabbed a bag of barbecue pork rinds off the shelf and set it down on the counter before walking over to the drink cooler.

"You get that differential unlocked yet?"

"Nope. I gave Terry a call, see if he could come down and help me with it, but he's down in Morgantown for the Fourth, so I'm screwed till at least Thursday." Bud walked back over to the counter and set down a quarter gallon of iced tea. He pulled his wallet out of his back pocket by its chain and threw several bills down on the counter then opened the pork rinds and cracked open the tea.

Tripper gathered up his food and then leaned in toward the counter slightly. "Do you know if Fallingwater is still open or is it gonna be closing soon?"

"Oh, you mean Rising Mildew?" Bud chuckled and took a drink.

For the first time Tripper looked over at Bud. He stood and easy foot taller than Tripper with a scruffy beard and Mossy Oak baseball cap. His t-shirt and jeans were stained and covered in years of grease and dirt. He had been outside working up until recently.

Tripper looked back at Hank with a grin. "Oh, is that what you guys call it?"

"That's what old Eddy Kaufmann called it," Bud interjected, "on account of Frankie Wright didn't know shit about shit and didn't have the contractors properly waterproof the son of a bitch."

Hank smiled at Bud and turned toward Tripper, "They're closed through the rest of the week. How long you stayin'? Might be able to catch it Mondey."

"Damn," Tripper dropped his head and looked down at his drink then looked back up at Hank. "I was hopin' to be able to head there today. I'm only stayin' at Jellystone tonight and then I gotta take off tomorrow morning to meet some family over in Gettysburg."

Bud tapped Tripper on the shoulder with the back of his hand, "Have you been watchin' that shit on PCN?" He turned toward

Hank and shook his head as he spoke. "I swear to god I don't know how I've lived in this state my entire life and knew so damn little about the Battle of Gettysburg. Our Dad took us there *every summer* as kids and I don't know half this shit they're talkin' about! You know they don't know where Bobby Lee's headquarters were? I was always told it was that god damn stone house with the little old woman on the rockin' chair and here they don't have a god damn *clue* where it was! Could 'uh been here or maybe it was clear over there! Doesn't make any damn sense. I thought park rangers and history people were supposed to be smart 'n shit."

"Yeah, I'm sorry, kid." Hank smiled but there was a tinge of sadness in his voice. "But, hey, it gives you a reason to come back, right?'

Tripper smiled, "Sure thing," with a nod. He started to make his way toward the door.

"Aw, man. You don't have to take off." Bud called after him. "I'm just a big dumb jerk, you don't have to go."

"You can eat in here if you want," Hank gestured to where Tripper had been standing. "Bud here does it all the time."

"Sure do," Bud made a show of shoving a fistful of pork rinds into his mouth and smiled, crumbs falling down his shirt onto the clean floor.

Tripper pressed his back to the door and nodded toward the parking lot. "Nah, that's alright. Yogi and Boo-Boo are expecting me over at Jellystone."

Bud turned to Hank and laughed, "If he was really smarter than the average bear he wouldn't have bought one of your sandwiches."

Both Bud and Hank burst out laughing. Tripper smiled at them for a second then pushed open the door and stepped outside.

"See you around."

Hank flicked his invisible cigarette and gave Tripper a slight wave.

"See you around, guy," Bud said with a mouthful of pork rinds.

* * *

Tripper pulled under a tree in the vacant parking lot for the Bear Run Reserve and ate. The sandwich wasn't bad. He watched the passing traffic for about twenty minutes and didn't notice anything strange. Finally, he drove the last quarter mile down the road to entrance to Fallingwater. After looking up satellite views of the park he knew that he wouldn't be able to see the house from the visitor parking lot. He pulled into the empty parking lot and took a space near the path down to the building.

He got out of his car and walked a few feet down the path. The wet dog smell of rain rolled up off the parking lot. There wasn't much to see through the trees. Occasionally the breeze would sway the branches enough to catch a glimpse of the house. Tripper had begun to make the short distance up the path back to his car when he heard a car door slam. It was quickly followed by another. The wind died down long enough that he could hear two men talking. The sounds bounced off the trees and the hill, hiding their source. There was the sound of an engine starting and then tires on pavement. Tripper ran the rest of the distance up the hill and dove into his car. He crawled over into the passenger's seat and peered out the window toward the parking lot entrance, keeping his head down low. After a minute or so he saw a large white delivery van with a logo for Green Room Catering pass by heading towards the entrance to the park. Tripper waited several minutes to make sure that no one else was coming or going before he left.

He pulled back into his parking space under the tree in the Reserve parking lot. It was coming up on eight o'clock. The sun made it look more like four. There wasn't much traffic to watch. The occasional minivan or rusted out pick-up truck. Part of Tripper questioned what the hell he was doing there but he didn't leave.

At a little after eight his wait started to pay off. A black unmarked luxury sedan cruised calmly down the road toward Fallingwater. Twenty minutes later a black Hummer and two black sports cars passed by. After that, every few minutes for almost an hour several black high-end cars would arrogantly cruise by with tinted windows and overly polished hubcaps. Finally, a group of five racing motorcycles sped down the road, riders in leather racing jackets, each bike with a different flamboyant paintjob designed to resemble a costume of the Avengers: Captain America, Spider-Man, The Hulk, Thor and Iron-Man. Then, nothing.

Tripper debated with himself during the compensating car parade when to move in closer or whether he should move in closer at all. He didn't want to move in too quickly and be noticed, but he couldn't turn back without seeing for himself what was happening. He knew there was a criminal case in this. At least six dead bodies: five at the office, one in the basement. Three shooters, two with Obama and Biden masks, one with a freaky looking eagle head. Suspicious behavior. Mystery webcam feeds to Vegas. Potential robbery. Quite literal shady real estate deals. And a drug collection Hunter S. Thompson would be envious of. He took out his phone and set an alarm for midnight.

* * *

The once empty visitors parking lot was now overflowing. The sound of crickets and tree frogs was drowned out by the syrupy thump of bass drums and tinny squeal of guitars broadcast over a sound system. As Tripper crept his way down the path closer to the building he recognized that the song was *Float On* by Modest Mouse.

"These people are just gift-wrapping reasons for me to not like them now," Tripper thought to himself.

All the lights were on in the house. There was whooping and hollering and the sound of several people fucking on the second-floor terrace. Tripper stayed near the edge of the property and slinked through the darkness around to the back of the house. There was a large black limousine parked near the back door flanked by all five of the racing cycles. Someone ran out of the house and vomited over the sidewall. Modest Mouse gradually faded out and surfaced again as the opening lines to *Take Me Out* by Franz Ferdinand. Tripper made and expression he thought convenience store Hank would make if something confused him.

"This sounds like a middle school graduation party from 2004," he said aloud, confident that no one would be able to hear him.

Somewhere in between the music there was the faint sound of a camera shutter actuating. Tripper's eyes involuntarily widened, and he stood very still, waiting. The sound happened again. Then two more times in quick succession. The noise was coming off the hill behind him. He turned around and saw a quick flash as the mirror reflected the light from the house through the lens. There was a faint, soft glow of a LCD display screen and the outline of someone's face. Tripper edged his way around the parked limo and did his best to climb the hill. Dead leaves crunched under his foot loud enough to get the attention of the shadowy photographer, who stopped taking a picture mid click, sending a digital beep down the hill toward Tripper. Tripper could feel their eyes staring at him. He watched up the hill waiting for the person to move again. They didn't. After what felt like an eternity, Tripper finally blinked and opened his eyes and no longer saw the light glow or the felt the eyes upon him. He didn't know if the person had left or if they had never been there to begin with.

Tripper circled around the house and found a walkway leading to the house covered by a tiered roof. He pulled himself up onto the roof and knelt down using it like stairs to walk to the second-floor balcony. When he reached the top, he saw two men embraced like Turkish wrestlers on the opposite side of the balcony shoving each other around. There was a girl, who until recently had been dressed, lying unconscious on the ground covered in tattered clothing. The music inside died down again and the opening notes of *Mr. Brightside* filled the house. A dozen people or so inside let out a sound of surprise and appreciation that slowly crescendo-ed and broke when they started singing. Tripper hated everything.

He jumped down onto the balcony, slid around to the door and looked inside. The room was full of professionals both young and old in various states of undress. Wearing party hats, sunglasses and smeared with makeup. The smell of alcohol and perfume pouring out of the house was enough to knock out an Oscar after party. Tripper held his breath and feared getting a contact high just from pressing up against the house. A shirtless man in his late twenties wearing mirrored aviator sunglasses yanked a woman (who either was a prostitute or just living the dream) toward him by her arm. She let out a quick scream then was cut off as he shoved her face into his by the back of her head. He pressed into her face until she began to whimper and scream, then let go of her head and shoved her with all his force toward the wall. She slammed into the wall and stumbled, falling to the floor and laying half outside the house. Tripper instinctively jumped back away from her. She laughed and looked around as she heard his feet shuffle. Her eyes caught the dull reflection of light from his shoes and looked up at him.

"Hey, what are you doing out here?" she said with a cracked husky voice. She pulled herself up into a standing position, leaning against the wall for support and reached out toward Tripper with one hand. "C'mon inside."

Tripper said nothing and pulled himself away from her.

"What's a matter, baby? I'm nice. I don't bite. C'mon inside." She spoke in the disingenuous tone girls learned somewhere in junior high.

Tripper backed away from her, freeing his shirt from her grasp. Just then, a middle-aged man in a Motley Crüe concert t-shirt stepped outside and started to lift her into the air.

"No, wait," the girl smacked the guys arm weakly. "Hold on, baby, he has to come inside."

The man laughed and began to walk back inside carrying the girl. She grabbed a hold of the door jam and stopped them both.

"No."

"What?" the man said a little annoyed.

"Make him come inside."

"Make who come inside?"

"Him," the girl pointed into the dark where Tripper was standing, "He won't come inside and it's making me sad," she pouted.

Motley Crüe held the girl in one arm and reached into the dark and grabbed Tripper with the other. "C'mon, man, just get in the fucking house." He pulled Tripper into the stream of light coming through the door way and looked him in the face then stopped. "Who the fuck are you?"

Tripper panicked and froze.

"Who the fuck *are* you?" he asked again, more angry than confused. He looked at the girl, "Who the fuck is this guy?"

"He was mean to me," she pouted again.

"You know him?"

"No."

Motley Crüe dropped the girl and drug Tripper into the house by his collar. Tripper grasped at the man's hands and kicked trying to slow himself down.

"HEY! ANY OF YOU FUCKS KNOW WHO THE HELL THIS IS?" Motley Crüe screamed over the music.

Several heads turned toward Motley Crüe, staring at Tripper like hungry coyotes.

"What the fuck is he doing here?" came a male voice from deep in the room.

"You know him?" said Motley Crüe, furious.

"I know he's not supposed to be here," said another voice.

"Who the hell is he?" demanded Motley Crüe.

"He's about to be fuckin' dead!" said the first male voice.

"No, don't kill him!" cried the girl in the doorway. For the first time, Tripper was thankful she was there.

"Well, what the fuck are we supposed to do with him?" asked Motley Crüe.

"Somebody get Bobby," called another voice.

A there was a collective "Ooooo" over the crowd and shuffling of feet as Tripper heard loud thunderous footsteps behind him. Motley Crüe gave Tripper and evil looking smile and head-butted him hard but good. Tripper fell to the ground like a rag doll and clutched his face. He was on the ground for only a moment before another smaller set of hands reached down and lifted him into up with a jerk. He took his hands off his face and opened his eyes long enough to see knuckles tattooed with the message "H8TE" rocket at his face, sending another sharp white pain through his head. Tripper started to collapse but was stopped short by two sets of hands that drug him by the shoulders out of the room.

When the pain was dull enough to see again, Tripper opened his eyes to discover that he was in what was designed to be a small modest family kitchen, but was now filled with young professionals and wannabe gang bangers. They all stood around a table covered in piles and baggies of powders, pills, and fake moss. A set of scales sat in the middle of the table and one gang banger in an oversized Biggie Smalls shirt and a leather racing jacket sat in front of it weighing something out.

"Lil' bitch muh'fuckuh thought he had the right to just sneak duh fuck een!" said one of the people holding him who was vary obviously white.

Tripper took in a deep breath and coughed on blood.

One of the wannabe gang bangers standing next to the table picked up a .45 semi-automatic off a counter, covered from end to end in liquor bottles, and walked over to Tripper.

"Lil' bitch ass muh'fuhckuh."

Tripper felt a pain in his head unlike anything he had ever previously experienced. A pain both dull and sharp exploded across the top of his head and shot down his spine to his pelvis as all the air was sucked out of his lungs. His entire body went limp and he was conscious long enough to watch himself vomit all over the floor.

CHAPTER ELEVEN

Hangover 1/1/83

Tripper woke up to the taste of bile in his mouth. He was in a sitting position with his face pressed against the wall. It took him most of a minute to recover from coughing after trying to take a deep breath. He shut his eyes tightly and opened them again, blinking several times. He was in a small room. The sounds of the party rose and fell outside of the door, but a good distance away. Occasionally he would hear footsteps approaching the door, but they would always thankfully turn away at the last moment.

After several minutes of struggling with his bindings, he became aware that he was not alone in the room. Directly in front of him on the opposite side of the room was a large, black ominous looking creature standing motionless on the wall, its body perpendicular to the floor. Everything inside of Tripper, except for his heart, stopped functioning. The creature could still tell he was there. He could smell him.

The figure continued to stare at Tripper. It stood silently on the wall, its feet never moving, and the muscles in its legs never bending from stress. Tripper stared back, fearing what it might do if and when he closed his eyes. He had no trouble keeping his eyes open, until he began to focus on it. He wondered how long it had been since he last blinked. Heat began to spread across his eyes and down to the back of his nose. His heartbeat quickened, thudding through his chest and into the wall he was leaning against, sending vibrations along the wall like primitive echo location. There was no way the figure didn't know he was still alive. Tripper was finally met with the choice to either hold his breath and suffocate, or be killed in whatever fashion this mysterious figure had dispatched thousands of victims before him. He decided a man's death was best and shut his eyes tightly as he sucked in his last gulp of air.

With his eyes shut, Tripper braced for impact. After a few seconds, he began to think how cruel it was that this figure would torture its victims by not immediately jumping on them when their eyes were closed. Maybe it attacked on the flipside, when its victims opened their eyes hoping that its monstrous greasy black visage be the last thing they saw before they died. So, with as much gusto as Tripper had decided to close his eyes, he once again opened them.

For the first time in he didn't know how long, Tripper was fully aware of the position of his body. With great effort he slowly lifted his head, feeling the carpet fibers pull away from the indentations they had made in his face. His legs were asleep, along with his right arm which he was three quarters laying on. He tried to move his hands to help lift himself up and realized they were bound together. After a few minutes he managed to wake up his legs enough to help him sit up. It was during this time, that his vision fully came into focus revealing to him the figure that had scared him for what seemed like hours; a large stack of chairs sitting in the corner on the opposite side of the room.

Slate blue early morning light crept in through the windows above him. It seemed cold for July, but Tripper told himself that he had been lying on the floor. Things seemed eerily still in the house, considering the mid-century style bacchanalia the previous night. The occasional bird chirped outside, and a dying small electric turbine motor whined and choked somewhere inside the house. Past that, all quiet on the western front.

With a great amount of cooperation from his legs and mental review of several *Bourne* movies, Tripper managed to stand. He leaned his forehead against the cool glass and looked out over the falls, then slowly panned around the property searching for signs of movement as he tried to loosen his hands from the rope behind his back.

The black limousine was gone. As were the racing cycles parked on the walkway. He stared for several minutes at the guest house on the back of the property. No one went in or out and nothing moved inside. Tripper was fully satisfied that he was alone.

However, internally Tripper regretted not being a boy scout and the cold sweat on his hands didn't do much to help untie his wrists. He would pull one end, increasing the tension and pressure on his wrists then would fumble with the fingers of his other hand to alleviate the pressure before his hands went numb. The harder he worked the harder he pressed his face into the glass. He tried to get a mental image of what the rope looked like around his wrists.

"If Maniac McGee can do it, Tripper Mayhew can do it too," he thought.

Tripper took a deep breath and closed his eyes then started his work again. He discovered in high school that in times of deep concentration he would begin humming *Champagne Supernova* to himself. He carried a great sense of personal shame over his brain's choice of working music, but if it worked then it worked, and he tried not to think about it too much. Before he knew it, the rope slowly slithered down his hands and fell to the floor.

Tripper walked out of his chair filled prison and in three steps entered the kitchen. The floor was littered with crushed snack foods, white powder and marijuana crumbs. Most of the bottles that covered the counter top by the sink were missing. What few bottles remained contained barely a swallow. The kitchen table that had been surrounded by old men and suits and young men in leather jackets and oversized t-shirts was now empty. The baggies of drugs and stacks of money, and scales were all gone, replaced with a small empty vase in the middle of the table. After standing in the doorway for a moment, the refrigerator kicked on and Tripper again became aware of the sound of the dying turbine motor which came from beyond the door and somewhere deeper in the house. Over top of the whine, he heard shallow labored breaths.

Tripper's eyes darted to the counter by the sink, where one of the oversized t-shirt thugs set down his gun, and saw nothing. A quick bolt of panic shot through him and he began to look around the kitchen for anything that could be used to defend himself.

"The Kaufmann's weren't very big on knives apparently," he said under his breath.

Frustrated after going opening several empty drawers in search of a knife, Tripper took a coffee mug from the kitchen counter, dumped out the cigarette ashes, and made his way to the door.

Tripper had seen college parties that had incurred less damage than what he saw in the main room of Fallingwater. The smell of alcohol, sweat, marijuana and semen were overpowering. Red plastic cups, drug paraphernalia and food covered every available surface. One couch was over turned. Throw pillows and used condoms littered the room like animals dropped dead in a heat wave. The entire front of the fire place was covered in a layer of black soot that reached the ceiling. A fur blanket lay on the floor in the middle of the room with stains in a rainbow of colors. On top of the fur, a naked girl no older than sixteen laid on her back looking around the room with wide spaced-out eyes, her neck covered in bruises and her make-up smeared, grinding her teeth, making the sound of a dying box fan. A large naked middle-aged man was on top of her, barely moving his hips as he thrust into her and breathed like he was running a 5K. Somewhere in the room *Almost Cut My Hair* by Crosby, Stills, Nash & Young played low and echoed off the tile.

On a couch parallel to the rug, sat Carson Pembroke, in an unbuttoned wrinkled white oxford, black and green harlequin pattered boxers and dress socks. He chewed and puffed on a cigar as he sat staring at the scene in front of him with no more emotional commitment than if he was watching the evening news.

"Umm...the *fuck*?" Tripper asked in a mild form of shock as he gestured to the man on top of the girl.

"Tripper!" replied Pembroke with a slight glance up, before he returned to watching the illegal act in front of him. "I wondered when you would wake up. Would you like some breakfast?"

"The fuck?" Tripper said more insistent as he gestured to the floor.

Pembroke looked up from the scene and over at Tripper and raised both eyebrows. "What? Do you want a turn?" He stood up and walked over to the man on top of the girl, placed one foot in his ribs and shook. "Hey, Jake," Pembroke spoke to the man as if he were a sleeping dog. "Jake, get off. The kid wants a turn."

"No, I don't!" said Tripper. "What the fuck is going on here? How old is she? Get him the fuck off!"

Pembroke turned from the man back to Tripper and shrugged.

"He paid his money."

He turned away from the two, walked back over to the couch and sat down.

"One of these days, you will learn the true value of a dollar."

Tripper watched the whole thing slack jawed before running over to the man and kicking him square in the forehead. The man lifted both hands, which he was using to hold his balance, and grabbed his face, leaving him to fall on top the girl. The girl let out a small quick bark then continued to groan. The man couldn't make any distinguishable words and slowly began to cry like an infant. Pembroke pulled the stubby cigar out of his mouth and threw it over the flailing couple into the fireplace before picking up a new cigar off the couch and lighting it.

Mimicking Pembroke, Tripper placed his foot on the man's ribs and, with a great amount of effort, managed to push the man off the girl. He then knelt down and wrapped the fur blanket around the writhing naked girl, glaring up at Pembroke. With one arm, he lifted her into a sitting position and the other he aimed the coffee mug up to Pembroke, pointing it at him like a gun.

"What's your problem, Mayhew?"

Tripper could still feel the adrenaline pump through him with each beat of his heart. Pembroke looked back at Tripper, still holding his lighter as he rolled his eyes around the room and shrugged. The man rolled around in front of the fireplace bawling like a little girl.

"You always were a dower son of a bitch."

"The last I knew of you, you were gathering flies in an Allegheny County morgue."

"Ahh, c'mon, hotshot, you're still trying to get over that? Mr. Movie Buff can't think of any way someone could fake their own death? Oh, that's right. You ran away like a little bitch once you heard gunfire."

"It's called self-preservation."

"When I was in school, it was called being a pussy."

Pembroke tossed the lighter onto the couch next to him and stared coldly down at Tripper. Tripper's mind raced as he tried to think of an escape. The girl writhed like a greased pig inside of the fur, groaning away, her eyes spinning around the room like a pinball machine. She smelled like piss. After a moment, Pembroke's face fell, and he shook his head rubbing his eyes with one hand.

"Seriously, Tripper, what the hell are you going to do?"

"First, I'm gonna call the fucking cops."

Pembroke rolled his eyes as he looked back at Tripper. "Yeah, then what?"

"What do you mean, then what?"

"Jesus Christ, Tripper, you are fucking stupid. I shouldn't have scored you so high in knowledge on your review."

Tripper was a little hurt by this, but he didn't immediately know why. Part of him wanted to interrogate Pembroke further, but he decided against it. Instead, he tightened his grip around the girl and began to slowly lift her and himself to their feet. Pembroke watched as Tripper and the girl began to back toward the door. Again, he shook his head in a combination of disappointment and disgust. He shoved his hand down between the couch cushions and pulled out a double barrel sawed-off Mossberg 12 gauge and set it down on the cushion next to him. By the looks of the piece it had been around for a while. Tripper instantly froze.

"I believe I asked you a question earlier, Mr. Mayhew. I would like it answered."

Tripper struggled to speak, still holding the mug on Pembroke. The girl remained oblivious and writhed in his arm. Jake, having tuckered himself out, laid snoring in front of the fire place.

"Can...can you repeat the question?"

"What are you going to do after you call the cops?"

Tripper searched for an answer, but could think of nothing. Instead, he began to wonder how far he would be able to get dragging a moaning, naked minor before he himself would be arrested for kidnapping and child molestation. That was, of course, considering that he would make it out of the building unventilated.

Then softly, almost courteously, came the sound of a gun being cocked and a familiar voice. Pembroke looked down at the shotgun sitting on the couch next to him, and then attempted to look behind himself out of the corner of his eye.

"Top of the morning, Pembroke", Montana said coolly.

Montana stood behind the couch dressed in all black, holding a Glock Model 19 in her leather gloved hands. Her clothes bore no logos, and her hair was pulled back and tied behind her head. She stood confidently holding the gun on Pembroke. "I believe you know why I'm here."

Pembroke remained relatively calm, albeit a little bit annoyed. "You know, I had a feeling about you."

"Yeah?" said Montana, "Thanks for the feedback. Where is it?"

"Where's what?"

Montana pressed the gun into the back of Pembroke's head.

"Don't get cute with me. Where is it?"

"Remind me what you're talking about."

Tripper stood watching in silence. After a moment, he looked down at his hand and realized that he let the mug drop. He looked back up at Pembroke, set his jaw and lifted it again.

"Wright-Kaufmann Agreement," Montana said flatly. "Where is it?"

"I don't know," replied Pembroke, making no effort to sound like he wasn't lying.

"Bullshit."

Pembroke shrugged and rubbed his hands together like a real estate agent. "I don't know what to tell you."

Montana moved the gun to the right of Pembroke's head, far enough that he would not be in the path of the bullet, and fired one round into Jake who somehow managed to slump from a laying position. Pembroke jumped and grabbed his ear with his hand, knocking the shotgun onto the floor in the process. The writhing girl let out a quick bark similar to when the now deceased Jake fell on top of her. Montana moved the gun back towards Pembroke's head and tracked it as he fell over on the couch.

"Do you know what to tell me now?" she asked calmly.

Pembroke said nothing but expletives for about half a minute. Montana took this opportunity to walk around to the front of the couch, aiming the gun the whole time. With one foot she kicked the shotgun away from the couch and towards Tripper. Tripper could see blood seeping through Pembroke's fingers from the other side of the room.

"Alright. Jesus Christ. You didn't have to shoot Larson. He didn't do anything."

"I can see where *you* might consider fucking children nothing, but most of the rest of the world doesn't."

"She liked it. She begged for it."

"I don't doubt." Montana held the gun right in Pembroke's face. "But I'm not going to. Where the fuck is it?"

Pembroke looked up at Montana from under his brow. "I never noticed that you were this cute before. Maybe it's only when you're angry."

Montana pulled back her arm and cracked Pembroke in the face with the butt of her gun. There was a hollow smacking sound, followed by a crack. Pembroke grabbed his nose and screamed into his hand. Tripper raised both eyebrows and nodded. He wanted to clap but both of his hands were occupied. He also thought it might have been distracting.

The girl wrapped in the fur had stopped her persistent buzzing whine. She began trying to nuzzle into Tripper's neck as he held her with one arm and held the mug on Pembroke with the other. She was whispering something to him, but he couldn't hear over Montana pistol-whipping Pembroke. He moved his ear slightly towards her as he strained to hear.

"Huh?" he asked low.

Her whispers were shallow and faint, which came as no surprise to Tripper since the entire time he had known her she had been making some sort of noise.

"...Molly," her voice crackled, and her mouth moved like she just came out of cryo-freeze.

"Your name is Molly?" Tripper was trying to suss out what she was saying while trying to listen to the other conversation in the room and be back up for Montana.

"Molly...Molly Lolly."

"Molly Lolly?"

"Molly Lolly Dolly."

"Molly *Lolly Dolly*?"

"Molly Dolly, daddy."

"I'm not your daddy. Whoever he is."

"Please..." she sounded more pained and insistent when she spoke.

Tripper unlocked his stare on Pembroke and turned to face the girl. Something inside him was telling him there was something very wrong. He moved in closer and whispered to her, asking what was wrong.

"Touch me...touch... touch my princess parts, daddy. Touch..." Tripper pulled his ear away from her and shook his head in disgust.

"Montana," Tripper said, forgetting that she was holding a gun on the man who was both his boss and supposed to be dead.

"What?" Montana shot back, a little bit more than annoyed.

"This chick," he said, wishing he had left the girl on the floor, "she's acting really fucking weird. I don't know what she's on, but I think we need to get her to a hospital."

Montana gritted her teeth and adjusted her grip on the Glock. Her eyes stayed locked on Pembroke's forehead as she spoke. "Tripper. If you talk to me *one more time* about that trippin' bitch, I'm gonna shoot her in the *fucking face* and *skull fuck* you with her."

Tripper raised both eyebrows and lifted his hand holding the mug in defeat. His eyes moved from Montana back to Pembroke. Then, slowly, he moved his hand from around the girl's shoulders and wrapped it around her still moving mouth.

Montana stepped closer to Pembroke and shoved the Glock in his face. She balled up her left fist and hit Pembroke dead center of his bleeding ear. Pembroke clutched his ear with both hands and fell over on the couch again.

"Is your ear ringing?" asked Montana, spitting as she talked.

Pembroke said nothing; just clenched his teeth in pain. After a moment he managed to speak.

"It's...it's in the guest house," Pembroke said with great effort. His throat sounded full and he kept spitting blood.

Montana grabbed a hold of the back of the couch with her punching hand and lifted her left foot over Pembroke's head, stomping down on him with her boot in time with her words. "Wrong-answer-Pembroke," she said, her voice becoming filled with sadistic glee. "Unlike you, asshat, I can do this all fucking day. Now this time," she shoved the barrel of the Glock in his mouth, "answer...*correctly.*"

Pembroke looked up at her like a caged rat. Somewhere on a soul level he gave up. His entire body went limp.

"It's not fun having foreign objects shoved inside you against your will, is it?" Montana asked in mock reassurance.

Pembroke said something around the gun that sounded like a dog about to vomit. Montana pulled the gun out of his mouth.

"Hmm?" she asked politely.

"Staircase bookshelf."

Montana took a few steps back from Pembroke, her gun aimed at his face. She picked up the sawed-off and walked over to Tripper who was still holding the mug on his boss. Montana ripped the mug out of his hand and threw it on the floor before wrapping his fingers around the Mossberg and aiming it at Pembroke.

"Stay with me. If he moves…" she looked Tripper dead in the eye as she spoke. Tripper looked back at her and nodded. He listened as she walked off behind him and began ascending the stairs, her footsteps fading into the upper recesses of the house.

It was unsettlingly quiet on the main floor of Fallingwater. Tripper listened to Pembroke's wet raspy breaths as he struggled to breathe. The writhing minor he was still holding with one arm had fallen silent and began to drool through his fingers. Tripper considered dropping her, but he feared that it would alert Montana and screw things up worse than they already seemed to be going.

"I think my lung's collapsed," Pembroke mumbled out loud.

"I think talking counts as movement, Pembroke," Tripper said flatly.

"Here we go," groaned Pembroke. "Five minutes in the presence of guns and you're already talking like a bad ass."

"No, I've always been a dower son of a bitch remember? Only now you take me seriously."

"I could never take your seriously, Mayhew. You've got less of a backbone than my son."

"Is that supposed to upset me?"

"I don't care how you feel about it. It's the god damn truth."

"Be that as it may, I really don't think that right now is the best time to be pissing me off."

"You're not gonna do shit, Tripper. You weren't shit before you started at LMJ and you're not gonna be shit now. I don't care what the piece of ass with the piece of iron says. You should have stayed in school. You should have gone for an actual engineering degree and not whatever pissant community college degree you got over the summer while you fucked some co-ed in the stairwell," Pembroke sucked in a stuttering lungful of air, glaring at Tripper as he bled. "Hard work, dedication, initiative, intuition. None of these things come to you naturally, Mayhew. And it's too late in life for you to learn them. Coda is a fuck up because I let him be. You're a fuck up because that's who you are. Stop thinking that you will ever be anything more than a number. You won't. You are a product of near poverty level upbringing and to hope that you will ever be anything more than that is not only laughable, it's pathetic. Give. It. Up."

Tripper pulled both triggers simultaneously. The main room of Fallingwater echoed with the sound of the blast and then fell silent. Pembroke laid motionless, the last remaining scraps of his brain slowly dripping onto the floor. Tripper's breathing remained steady and even, but his heart pounded like a prize-winning race horse. The naked girl once again had become conscious with the sound of the blast and began whimpering like a small child. Tripper paid no attention.

After a moment, Tripper became aware of the sound of pages turning somewhere behind him. He turned around and saw Montana with a furrowed brow, holding a large storage envelope in her arm as she licked the bare fingers of her free hand and flipped through a stack of papers. She said nothing for moment then addressed Tripper without looking up from the document.

"Ready to go?" she asked with all the mock enthusiasm of a camp counselor.

Tripper tried to shake himself out of the daze.

"I'm sorry I- "

"Don't be," replied Montana in a business-like voice. "You should see some of the shit he's done."

Tripper looked from Montana, to Pembroke's lifeless mangled corpse, back to Montana. Montana flipped through a few more pages then, seemingly satisfied, slipped the document back into the storage folder.

"Ready to go?" she asked again, this time looking him straight in the face.

"Yeah," Tripper said simply.

Montana clicked her boots together before turning on her heel and heading for the door. Tripper followed behind, dragging the whimpering unconscious minor with him. As they stepped out the back door, Montana was talking in Japanese on her cell phone. She opened the door and dropped it, forgetting Tripper was behind her then caught the door and held it for him. Tripper wondered how they were going to leave since he didn't see any vehicles parked outside earlier. Just then he heard the chirp of a car alarm and saw the flash of headlights, as Montana opened the driver's side door of a late model Buick Verano. She was hanging up the phone as she began to step into the car. Tripper waited for her to pocket her phone before he spoke.

"Where do you want me to put her?" he asked.

"The falls," Montana said flatly.

Tripper looked at her confused. Montana was about to sit down when she realized that Tripper hadn't moved. She looked at him, raised one eyebrow and cocked her head to the side.

"Leave her?" she said, unsure as to why he was still standing there.

"Should we really leave an unconscious, intoxicated minor at the scene of a multiple homicide?"

"Why not? She didn't do it."

Tripper adjusted the weight of the girl leaning against him. "I really think we should get her to a hospital. She was making some weird noises earlier."

"Like a dying box fan?"

"Yeah."

"Yeah, she's on molly. That happens."

Tripper gave Montana a concerned look. Montana looked back at Tripper, wondering why he hadn't come to the conclusion to leave her, too. After a moment of awkward silence, Montana dropped her head and rolled her eyes, popping the trunk with the car keys. Tripper walked around to the back of the car and laid the unconscious girl inside, once again covering her up with the stained fur rug. As he slammed the trunk, he noticed that Montana was standing next to him. She stared blankly at Tripper for a moment then pulled the Glock out of the holster from under her jacket and randomly fired three shots straight down into the trunk of the car. Tripper jumped back away from the gunfire and stumbled having to stop himself from falling several times. He stared terrified at the bullet riddled trunk hatch, then looked at Montana. The sound of the shots echoed through the woods.

"What the fuck was that about!"

Montana calmly re-holstered her weapon and walked to the front of the car.

"Air holes."

CHAPTER TWELVE

Car Thief

The Buick rocketed back towards Allegheny County with Montana at the wheel and Kaleida in the speakers. Tripper sat in silence, dumbstruck, occasionally looking over at Montana. It was strange being in an enclosed vehicle alone with any co-worker, but it was especially strange now. Montana's intensity was enough to fill the car all on its own. Tripper carved out his own space and pressed himself tight against the door.

A little after nine o'clock, Montana guided the car down Smallman Street in the Strip District. She pulled into a space in front of a sandwich shop and parked the car facing the store front. Tripper sat with his head in his hand, massaging his forehead with his thumb and index finger.

"We're stopping, I guess?" he said with more snark than he intended to.

Montana took the keys out of the ignition and dropped them into a pocket on her jacket. She twisted the rearview towards her and checked her reflection. She brushed a few stray hairs out of her face as she spoke. "Wait here. I'll be back in a few minutes."

Tripper glanced over at her, turning his head only slightly. With no further words Montana picked up the folder sitting in the center console, opened her door and stepped out of the car. Tripper looked dead ahead and watched Montana's movements in the reflection of the sandwich shop window. She walked to the back of the car and rustled around in the trunk for a few minutes before slamming it shut and taking off for the building on the opposite side of the street with quick sharp steps.

The morning was quiet in the strip. It was as if whatever strange sense of calm that had covered Fallingwater earlier that morning had followed Montana and Tripper back to the city. The stillness crept around the corners of the buildings and down the sidewalk with feline caution. Cigarette butts and plastic cup lids skittered in the occasional breeze. Tripper turned toward his window and looked west down Smallman Street. The amber sun of morning was still creeping over St Stanisalaus, sliding down the road like something out of a 90's car commercial. The SS Natchez chugged down the Allegheny River and let out a long yawn of its horn, echoing through the city, waking up anyone within earshot so they wouldn't miss the morning.

Montana opened the driver's door and sat down. She dropped an orange safety pop in Tripper's lap and started the car. With a readjustment of the review and a quick glance, she backed out of the parking space and took off west down Smallman.

Tripper picked up the safety pop and looked from it, to Montana, and back. She was sucking on one of her own, its pathetic rolled paper ring sticking out between her lips. Tripper watched as she squinted her ice blue eyes, the purple skin under them wrinkling as she crinkled her nose, knitted her jet-black eyebrows together and ripped the stick out of her safety pop and rolled down her window, tossing it out. Wild stray hairs blew across her face in the wind and she brushed them away with one hand. She adjusted her tight grip on the wheel. Tripper, once again, was at a loss for words.

They drove out of the city, back through the Fort Pitt tunnels re-tracing the route Tripper had drove less than twenty-four hours earlier. As they got closer to Robinson, he became more nervous. He was beginning to realize that despite everything he had seen, he in fact knew very little and it was enough to make him just north of anxious to be back there again.

Montana exited onto South Hampton and switched on her turn signal, clicking in the direction of LMJ. Tripper felt like he was either going to throw up his heart, or have it get stuck in his throat and choke to death. He could feel his face get hot and his pulse throb in his neck. An involuntary spasm shot through his jaw and causing him to grind his teeth. Slowly, he began to raise his hand like he was in grade school. Then, just a block away from the grey collar crime scene, Montana flipped on her turn signal again and turned into the parking lot of the Doyle Inn and Suites. Tripper itched the side of his nose.

The Buick drove around the parking lot and slipped out of sight into the guest parking garage under the building. Montana picked a spot near the glass box that housed the elevator and parked the car.

"This is us," she said under her breath.

* * *

Montana slid the key card into the lock of room 315 and stepped inside, Tripper close behind. The suite was large enough to sleep five people comfortably. Montana bee-lined for the phone on the nightstand between the two queen-sized beds pressed up against the western wall. The morning light glowed through the sheer white curtains creating a halo of white around her untamed black hair. A rather large black leather couch was pressed up against the wall on the opposite side of the room from the beds. Montana moved the mouthpiece of the phone away from her face and pointed.

"The couch is comfortable," she said. Her words were more of a strong suggestion than a friendly review of the room's amenities.

Tripper gave a resigned shrug and sat down on the couch with a sigh. It was comfortable. Montana lifted the phone to her mouth and spoke.

"Yes, would it be possible to place an order to room service?"

Tripper scanned around the room taking it all in. Sitting on a specially made side table against the South wall between two floor to ceiling windows, was a modest sized flat screen TV. Perpendicular to it was a desk about four feet long holding three ammo boxes and several file folders all neatly stacked and arranged. In the middle was a green silicone mat surrounded by items from a gun cleaning kit.

"Explains the Do Not Disturb sign," Tripper thought.

Montana dug through a black luggage case that lay across the still made bed farthest from the window. She glanced across the room at

Tripper staring at her work station and picked the remote control up off the nightstand.

"Yes, that'll be all. Thank you."

Montana tucked a set of clothes under her arm and walked across the room to Tripper, handing him the remote. Tripper stared at the remote like an ancient relic, and then looked up at Montana.

"You can watch TV if you want."

"What would you like on?" he asked slowly, taking the remote.

"*You* can watch TV. *I'm* getting in the shower. Alone."

Montana stared at Tripper and sucked on her lips, pressing them tight against her teeth, outlining her fangs.

"Alright," Tripper said in an easy going way.

Tripper flipped on the TV as he heard the shower turn on in the bathroom. He went through the channels in a sort of daze until he found *The Big Lebowski*. He was just in time to miss *The Man in Me*, but soon enough to catch Donnie's first strike. Most of the way through the Chinaman speech, he heard a knock at the door.

"Room service," came a muffled male voice through the door.

Tripper looked around the room in a sort of panic. He glanced at the sliding door that led to the bathroom, the faint sound of water over a ventilation fan in the ceiling.

"Hold on a second."

He stepped up to the door and for the first time in his life used the peep hole. There was a middle-aged man in a white dress shirt with a name tag standing outside. Tripper opened the door and let the man in. He wheeled a large cart into the room and directed it towards the desk in front of the television. With all the care of a footman, he set a metal bottomed glass mug full of hot tea in the middle of the green silicone mat. He picked up a small ceramic container and poured white liquid from it into the glass, leaving just enough headroom to drink. Then, without a word to Tripper, he wrapped up his cart and left, pulling the door closed behind him.

Walter was relating Jesus' torrid history to the Dude when Montana stepped out of the bathroom. She was wearing a California tourist t-shirt, grey loose-fitting yoga pants, and flip flops. With her hair still damp, she walked straight-backed over to her London Fog that sat steaming on the table in front of the TV. Montana looked at the TV blank-faced for a moment as she lifted the mug. She stared at the screen and glanced down at the table long enough to navigate menus on her phone with her free hand. All at once, she tapped her phone and took a slow smooth sip from the London Fog as the opening notes of Lana Del Rey's *Cruel World* echoed through the suite over the movie. As she slowly drank, and the music played, Montana's shoulders gradually dropped as if her entire body was sighing. Tripper calmly raised the remote and muted the television.

Montana closed her eyes and sighed after she swallowed, cradling the mug in her hands. She stood silent for a moment before turning toward Tripper. "I thought you would have been asleep by now," she said in a voice more familiar to Tripper than the one she had been using since he met her at Fallingwater.

"Still a little too wired for that. I'll crash eventually."

Montana stared at him like a scientist observing a deep-sea creature for the first time. Something inside of Tripper started the air raid siren; the rest of him was too tired to react. He felt like everything was moving in slow motion. Montana raised both eyebrows and tightened her lips.

"Hmm," she said flatly before taking another sip of her drink and turning to walk toward the bed closest the window.

"I suppose this is too late to be asking this," said Tripper, "but...what the hell is going on?"

"Your name is Tripper Mayhew," Montana said calmly as she turned down her bed, "you are in a room at the Doyle Inn and Suites on South Hampton Road in Robinson Township, Pennsylvania with a one Montana London, myself, a former co-worker of your former place of employment, LMJ Engineers."

"Ok," Tripper said nodding. "That's really about all that I understand."

"Well," Montana sat down on her bed with a bounce and let out a contented sigh, "that's about all I have to tell you. If there is anything else you are confused about you're going to have to be more specific in the phrasing of your question."

"Who are you?" Tripper felt himself slightly recoil from Montana as he asked the question.

"I'm Montana London, as I said," she continued in her same calm manner. Tripper almost wanted to call her attitude happy-go-lucky and coming from her, that scared him.

"Fine, then *what* are you? Who do you work for?"

Montana cocked her head to the side and chewed the inside of her cheek with one fang as she looked at Tripper. "It's not that I think you can't know, it's that I'm not the one to tell you."

"What's that supposed to mean?"

Montana slowly picked up her mug and watched Tripper from under her brow. "If you tell anyone that I told you what I'm about to tell you, I will be fired."

"I won't tell anyone."

"There is no job placement or workers comp if you get fired from this job. And I like my job. So, understand I am being extremely *gracious* and *reckless* in telling any of this to you."

Tripper crossed his heart with his right hand.

"I work for something, not a company, but something that is referred to as The Guild. It's not very old. It was established back in the late forties after World War II. There are many branches to it and they operate strictly in the United States. They are like the police that no one knows exists, but they are everywhere at once."

"What, like the Pinkerton Detectives?"

"Not quite. The Pinkerton's were sloppy for one, and stupid for two. The Guild is very smart and very clean, because they have to be. You know that saying, 'Who watches the watchman?'"

"Yeah."

"The *Guild* watches the watchman. The Guild is the people on the ground inside the town, with a set of binoculars, but they are more than just curious citizens. They keep the balance."

"The balance to what?"

"As much as they can. Their numbers have shrunk since 9/11 and they don't have the reach that they used to. But they are still out there."

"Why haven't I met any before you?"

"In all actuality, you probably have. Have you ever eaten at a restaurant? Pumped gas? Went to the movies? Worked at a large company? You've met them, but you didn't know you met them. That's the whole point."

Tripper stood up from the couch and walked over toward the bed. As he got closer to her, Montana turned her head away from Tripper and gave him the side eye as she held up one finger. Tripper stopped dead in his tracks and held up both hands.

"I'm not doing anything. I just don't want to yell across the basketball court you checked into to talk to you."

Montana used her eyes to guide Tripper towards one of the roll away ottomans tucked under the table. Tripper pulled one out and sat down. "What happened this morning?"

"You witnessed the reclamation of rightfully owned Guild property from the possession of Crystal Communications and Industrial Safety Engineers, as executed by a Guild member."

"Crystal and ISE?"

"Sound familiar?" Montana said with a drink.

"What do they have to do with this?"

"They are, in a word, evil." Montana tightened her lips and raised her eyebrows.

"I kinda figured that when I worked for them. Wait...what do you mean 'sound familiar'?"

Montana gave Tripper a sinister smile. Something Tripper felt was intended for Pembroke, but Montana didn't get to use earlier. "What do you think?"

A wave of cold shot through Tripper like a tuning fork. "What do you know about me?"

"A lot. I'd rather not go into it, so I'll just leave it at that."

Tripper wanted to escape Montana's frosty stare, but couldn't. Steam rose up from her drink like its namesake implied and danced in front of her fangs like a Universal Monster movie.

"Are you a vampire?" Tripper asked, terrified to the core.

Montana's face fell like the Sands Casino, only to be replaced by her standard issue deadpan stare. "Are you seriously asking me that?"

"You're being cryptic and defensive. And you're flashing your fangs at me like a god damn Anne Rice novel."

"I was fairly certain we had already established the reasoning behind my attitude, but apparently it didn't sink in. And as to my *teeth*, they're just *my teeth*, fuck you very much."

"Fine." Tripper crossed one leg over the other and gripped his ankle to keep it in place. He was happy that he had finally knocked Montana off her high horse. "Then why did you follow me to the museum the other day?"

"I could ask you the same thing."

"I didn't follow you. I was there to---," Tripper hesitated, "I was there on leisure."

Montana stared through him, "And I was there on business."

"Was it concerning this, what would you call it, case?"

"Yes. And yes." Montana sucked her tooth with her tongue.

They sat in silence staring at each other for a minute or two. They both recognized the need to let the hostile energy come down before they continued talking.

"What's going to happen to LMJ?"

"The building will be cleaned and scrubbed of all information related to LMJ Engineers and their work as a subsidy of ISE, and in three to eight months another company will move into it and set up their business. If not, it will sit empty for several years before it is demolished and something else builds on top of it."

"Who were the shooters?" Tripper dropped his leg and leaned forward.

"The individual in the Barack Obama mask was Hunter Musgrave---"

"Hence, Pembroke still being alive."

"---and the second shooter in the Biden mask was Coda Pembroke, Carson's son."

"Jesus," Tripper raised his eyebrows and turned toward the window, "where the hell has he been all summer?"

"Hospital," Montana said flatly then took a drink, "he was in a car accident back in May, shortly before his graduation from Penn State."

"Damn." Tripper thought for a moment. "Who was in the eagle mask?"

"That was me," Montana said softly, dropping her head.

"Why were you going to shoot me?" Tripper felt his voice rise without his permission.

"I was trying to scare you."

"It worked."

"Not well enough."

"What were you doing in the basement?"

Montana looked up from her drink and directly into Tripper's eyes with the goal-oriented drive of an EMT. Tripper's eyes were squinted and bloodshot. Montana bit her lip and looked out the window as she shook her head.

"You should get some sleep, Trip. You're fading fast."

"Can you answer this one thing?"

"I've answered a lot for you already," she stared down at her swirling drink. "That's all the more you need to know. Get some sleep."

Tripper stared at her for moment. Her demeanor had changed. As if he had hit upon a subject that he wasn't supposed to. He nodded slightly and looked down at his hands before standing up.

"On the couch," Montana added quickly. There was a pause as she gave Tripper an almost apologetic look from the corner of her eye. "If you don't mind."

Tripper walked over to the couch and laid down. He turned his face toward the back of the couch, not wanting to look at Montana and thinking Montana didn't want to look at him. After a few minutes, she got out of bed and walked over to the desk, turning off the music and un-muting *The Big Lebowski* as Walter invited the Dude to go bowling and then limped back to his car.

* * *

"Tripper. Tripper, wake up."

Montana stood over Tripper with a calm expression, but something in the room felt panicked. The light coming in through the windows was the dirty amber of the evening sun. A music video for Nada Surf and several episodes of *The Adventures of Pete and Pete* flashed through Tripper's head.

"What? What's wrong?" Tripper looked around the room, then rubbed his eyes and looked up at Montana.

"Take this."

Tripper saw something white in front of his face as his vision came into focus. It was a plain white business card with a black and white Profil "G" dead center on its face. Tripper carefully took it from Montana's hand and flipped it over. The back was a string of letters and numbers.

"What's this?" Tripper looked up at Montana scared and confused.

Her face slowly came into focus. Her ice blue eyes were sad and her normally up-curved lips were curved down. Tripper looked throughout the room for some sort of threat.

"What? What is it?"

There was the rising sound of running footsteps outside the door.

"Good-bye, Tripper."

The door to the room flew open and slammed into the wall, sending the handle vibrating furiously. Tripper continued to stare up at Montana who looked down at him with her disconcerting frown. Suddenly, he felt himself being lifted into the air and drug backwards off the couch. He heard a scream, which may have been his, and the sound of several men breathing heavily under masks. He looked down at his arms and the white gloved hands wrapped around them, that lead up to red, white, blue and yellow polka dotted bag suits. There was a quick flash of a giant red shoe over the cheap 60's inspired hotel carpet beneath him. Montana stood a-symmetrically framed in the door way, her sad expression echoing out of the room like a primitive bullhorn. There was the sound of moving fabric and a muffled gasp, then nothing.

CHAPTER THIRTEEN

Elastic Heart

Lottery machines went down statewide that night. Neighborhoods were choked with the sweet dirty smell of illegal fireworks. Somewhere up on Center Grange Road, a little red-haired girl and her red-haired father walked to the edge of their property and released a paper lantern into the moonlit sky. In a house near the VFD, someone forgot to turn off the TV in their grandmother's basement and a VHS copy of *Night of the Living Dead* played out to the color bars. Weekend warriors cruised past their old high school sporting flea market leather biker vests. Recent graduates of that high school stumbled into the woods, dropped acid and engaged in their first act of infidelity as adults. A dark-haired boy sat alone in his parent's bedroom listening to *Strange Days* and watching the fireworks across the street. Montana London found some old movie on TV and slept soundly.

Tripper Mayhew never made it home. No one saw him for four months. By the end of the summer his apartment door sported an orange piece of paper, but it had long since been emptied by persons unknown. Mid-November he interviewed at a private engineering firm and machine shop in Torrington, Connecticut. March of the next year he was gone. He wasn't sighted again until April at Coriander Business Park in Muncie, Indiana. Five years after the events at Fallingwater, he was checked into the Days Inn Lansing, Michigan.

He woke up that morning humming *Serve the Servants*. He figured it was decent enough morning music. The open indoor courtyard outside of his room echoed with the sounds of children splashing in the heated pool. Tripper considered calling the front desk but upon consulting the alarm clock discovered that they were well within the designated swimming hours. He had just slept late.

Tripper laid on his back flipping through his phone, tapped the screen and then set it back down on the nightstand. One of the three laptops in the room broadcast the unmistakable sound of Cobain's feedback and Tripper sat up in bed. The television displayed a window asking if he was still watching. He pressed a button on the remote, turning back on whatever show he fell asleep watching and then muted it. The recording software on his first computer flashed a red button in the lower right-hand corner. After oozing out of bed, he discovered that the laptop's SD card was full. The second laptop appeared to still be recording.

Tripper absent mindedly hummed along with the music as he fished an empty SD card out of a foam compartment of the hard-plastic luggage case on the floor and swapped it out with the full one in the first laptop. His body went through the motions, but his mind was still locked in his dream. Something about a hooded figure floating above the skylight of the hotel pool. The pool was filled with blood, of course, and there was another person in his room that he knew, but he couldn't see their face. The phone rang incessantly. He couldn't really remember what it was. It was just the type of dreams he had.

He held one headphone to his ear as he cued up the recording software again. With two fingers he parted the venetians and looked across the second-floor walkway and down at a room on the first floor parallel with the pool, about halfway across the building. The blinds were closed, but he could tell that the floor lamp in the room was still on. He lucked out that they checked into a room he could see from his. Over the headphone, all Tripper could hear was breathing.

He picked up a bright orange field survey notebook off the desk near the laptops and scribbled down a few notes including the time. On the second laptop, he pulled open a window displaying a video feed. He stopped the recording, saved the file and then played it at quadruple speed. Mike Ness had just started singing when he realized that he left his music player on shuffle. *Under My Thumb* rattled through the hotel room and Tripper was instantly reminded of Montana, who he had blissfully not thought about for quite some time. He hadn't seen her in about three years. Work had been keeping all Guild members in a near constant cycle of cases for the last several years, to the point that if you had any contact with other members it was pure happenstance. Monthly issues of the *Plainclothes Observer* reported the current number of Guild members along with updates of top cases, embezzlement hotspots (usually California and Florida, oddly enough) and articles featuring top members and their most recent exploits. Montana seemed to almost always be somewhere on those lists. What started out as pride upon seeing her name in the underground paper soon turned to bitter resentment. Not that she was doing better than him, but that she all but directly refused his invitations to talk over the last several years.

He felt betrayed. She brought him into this world, she was his sole reference and, as he learned later, instrumental in his becoming a member. In the beginning, he wanted to thank her. Now he wanted to tell her to go fuck herself. If she was just going to forget him upon joining, she had many opportunities to not involve herself as much as she did. Over the years, with experience, he learned that she was setting herself up to be his mentor, but she never stepped up. Tripper enjoyed his job, most of the time, but he felt alone. He knew no one. He couldn't talk to anyone he knew before and his only companionship came from cold impersonal conversations with hotel clerks, waiters, flight attendants, and over the phone with the Guild quartermaster. They didn't have to strike up a lifelong friendship, which he learned at LMJ Montana was virtually incapable of doing, but the least she could have done was say, 'Hi' when he saw her that one time or respond to a fucking email. As the song faded out, Tripper came to staring at the video playback which had ended. He had missed the whole thing.

* * *

Tripper went out that night. The microwave in his room worked fine and he had enough rations to last him at least two weeks before he would have to leave, but mentally he needed out. He walked past the brain dead front desk clerk and out into the chilly night air of Michigan summer. The area had been built up, he had been told, but it still looked pretty dead. Receipts blew through the parking lot. The area reminded him of home. A car drove by playing Ellie Goulding's *Anything Could Happen* at attention grabbing volume. Tripper took out his phone and checked the time. It was a little after eleven.

There was a suped up farmer's market across the eight-lane express way in front of the hotel that sold yogurt covered pretzels, which were widely regarded as a Schedule One narcotic by most Guild members. So much so, that many field offices held open orders for them and received multiple shipments a week. Guild members were, by and large a weird lot, and they took great pride and joy in exchanging odd snacks with one another that they discovered in the far-flung towns where they were often stationed. Chewy spicy ginger candy, cough medicine flavored pop, micro-brewed crème soda, apricot infused sour dough bread, spicy salsa made almost exclusively from cherries, and above all those god-damn yogurt covered pretzels. But the farmer's market was closed.

Tripper walked through the parking lot and headed east toward the relative center of Lansing. The lull in traffic due to the hour afforded him the opportunity to cross the expressway without stopping or looking up. A little less than a quarter of a mile away, he saw a sign for some all-night diner, its lights flickering and blinking like a halfhearted beacon. He shoved his fists in his jacket pockets and whistled *Mexican Radio* as he walked.

The parking lot only had a few cars in it. He thought to himself that it was most likely employees. The interior looked like an average all night diner you would find in the suburbs of any city along the interstate. A middle-aged man in dirty jeans, with a dirty flannel and a dirty plate sat at the counter nursing a cup of coffee. A girl about Tripper's age sat by herself in a corner with her back against the window, refusing to give up scene hair. The sign next to the hostess station read PLEASE SEAT YOURSELF and the smell of coffee and maple syrup filled the building like generic oxygen. Tripper's Doc Marten's clicked against the filthy broken tile on his way to a booth at the back of the restaurant. Adele's *Rumor Has It* crackled over the aged sound system.

Tripper sat down in a booth and slid across the tuck and roll that shined with the dull polish of use. He took in a deep breath through his nose and coughed before picking up his menu. After a minute or so he heard the familiar sound of flat-soled shoes and looked around for the waitress. A young woman in a new powder blue polo and brown slacks set down a glass of Coke on the table in front of Tripper and then pulled a note pad out of her black apron front. Tripper furrowed his brow in confusion and looked from the glass to the waitress.

"What can I get you, hun?" she said calmly.

"Pardon?"

"To eat," she looked over the note pad at Tripper. "Food?"

"Uhh…shouldn't you take my drink order first?" he said a little dazed.

"I got you one. Coke," she said with a smile.

"Ahh…I see that," Tripper looked at the glass and nodded once. "But I didn't order it."

"No," she continued to smile then looked down at her pad, "but I figured I owed you one."

Tripper felt like he had wandered into a dream he would have had when he was twelve. He held his hand up perpendicular to his face and pressed his thumb into the space between his eyebrows as he stared at the glass for answers. He finally submitted and folded his hands with his elbows propped on the table.

"Alright," he pressed his folded hands to his mouth and looked up at the waitress.

The waitress smiled and shook her head slightly. "You don't remember me at all do you? Hanrahan's?" She bent her arms at the elbows and held her hands out to her sides, shaking them in mock fanfare. "Cranberry Township. I spilled pop on your files once and invited you to a Christmas party."

Tripper's face dropped. "Cammy?"

"That's me!" she said, suddenly very excited.

"Wow, you've...," Tripper looked her up and down quickly then stared her in the face, "moved."

"I know," she said lolling her head to the side. "I've gained weight." She let out her familiar quick nervous laugh.

Tripper shook his head staring off into space. "No. No, can't say that. Just...wasn't expecting it."

Cammy began to roll into her nervous excited chatter, but something seemed a little more laid back about her now. There was a little more confidence in the way she moved and talked. Tripper was happy to see a familiar face, but his Spidey-senses wondered why it was this one.

"What brings you up here?" he began to speak more conversationally.

"Work," Cammy rolled her eyes and lolled her head in time with her response, "How's your work going?"

Tripper had just set down his glass and froze. He pulled back his jaw and bit his lip. "It's goin' alright, y'know. Steady, but..." He trailed off and looked at her.

Cammy smiled down at Tripper with her listening face. Tripper continued to suck on his lip and quickly raised his eyebrows one time. She lifted her left arm and pulled up the sleeve of her polo, exposing a tattoo of a snake eating its tail on in inside of her bicep. She looked from the tattoo to Tripper.

"Looks recent," Tripper nodded slowly.

"Eigh*teen* months," Cammy said proudly, then rolled down her sleeve.

"How do you like it?" he asked with a warm smile.

Cammy returned the smile. "I like it. It's good. Beats being a waitress." She laughed and then looked down at her outfit. "For a living," she rolled her eyes again.

Tripper nodded his head and looked back to his glass, "Good. Glad to hear it."

Cammy took his order with a smile and tucked the notepad back down in her apron. She had made it a few steps away from the table before she stopped and then walked back. Very coolly and confidently she bent down to eye level, leaning on his table with one arm.

She held her face less than an inch away from Tripper's and for the first time, he realized that Cammy's eyes were brown.

"I was supposed to give you a message," she said seriously.

Tripper's eyes darted for a moment. "Yeah? From who?"

"Can't say," she shook her head. "Two things. One: Tonight." She tapped on the table with one finger and pressed into it for emphasis.

Tripper searched her eyes as she spoke. "What the hell?" he thought, "I thought I had two more weeks." After a beat he asked her: "What else?"

Staring him in the eye, she shook her head, "Not anymore."

Their very brief but intense conversation hung in the air between them thicker than the smell of coffee and maple. Finally, Cammy slowly stood up and patted Tripper's hand in a gentle nurse-like way.

"Good to see you again, Tripper," Cammy turned and walked away.

"Good to see you too, Cammy." Tripper looked back to his condensing glass of caramel colored fizz and stared at it for a moment before taking a drink.

* * *

It took Tripper less than fifteen minutes to pack his room. He dropped the individually packaged and labeled SD cards into a bubble envelope and stuffed it in a hidden compartment in the hard-plastic luggage case. All the laptops had been packed except one, which he left laid out on the desk. He used the hotel's Wi-Fi to hack into the hotel's own servers and shut off all the security cameras. There was nothing on the laptop except for fake family photos and dummy business files for a company that didn't exist. The only software of interest left on the machine would be deleted either remotely, or hands on, after he activated it, at which point he would fry the motherboard. This was an emergency situation and he didn't know why. But he knew what to do.

A sweep of the building informed him that there were only three booked rooms, not including his own and the target. There was only one desk clerk on duty, no maintenance or cleaning staff. The target and his wife had taken three tabs of Valium at around 10:45 so they weren't going to hear anything. Tripper checked his service weapon, pulled on a black ski mask and took a deep breath before stepping out the door of his hotel room.

The empty indoor courtyard echoed with the sound of his closing door. The white Christmas lights wrapped around the fake palm trees glimmered off the pool's surface. Tripper slowly crept down the stairs to the main floor and walked over to the fire alarm on the wall. He placed his gloved hand on the pull bar and counted to three before pulling it.

The tinny high-pitched bell and dive alarm-like siren were instantly annoying. Tripper hid in the shadows under the stairs and watched the drama unfold. One after another, the three occupied rooms opened, and people stepped out to look around at the courtyard. The front desk clerk stepped into the courtyard and motioned for everyone to make their way to the front door with all the coolness of a frazzled teenager. A businessman, a couple, and a family of five slowly marched their way into the front lobby and out the door.

Tripper watched the desk clerk step outside before pulling his phone out of his pocket and tapping a button. The fire alarm shut off. The software on his computer that blocked the call to the fire department and police had been deactivated and then deleted. A domino program would begin frying the computer immediately. Tripper walked slowly out from underneath the stairs and made his way to the target room. He stopped in front of the door and took another deep breath. From over his shoulder he heard slow, cautious footsteps. He turned around and saw the desk clerk inching their way toward Tripper with wide fearful eyes.

"We've already called the police," the clerk's voice trembled. "Don't do anything dangerous. Just put...the gun...down."

Tripper quickly raised his gun and pointed it at the clerk's forehead. The clerk immediately froze and stared at the weapon. Tripper turned fully toward the clerk and began walking toward him with slow deliberate steps. The clerk turned and ran for the front door with Tripper giving chase and gaining ground. He soon realized that he would be able to outrun the clerk and slowed down a little bit to let him escape. He reached the automatic doors just in time for the clerk to slam them shut and lock them with a big ring of keys. Tripper pressed his face against the plexi-glass and crossed his eyes. He held the gun up to the small crowd outside and pointed at the Ramada Inn the next block over.

"Sorry, folks," Tripper said, doing his best to sound deranged. "No *va*cancies. Why don't you try THAT ho-tel across the *street*?" He nodded slowly, hoping to send the message home. The crowd stared at him with blank terrified expressions. Tripper began to tap on the plexi-glass with the butt of his gun in a clock rhythm. "*Tick, tock, TICK, tock, TICK, TOCK, TICK….*" The crowd finally took the hint and ran in the direction he had been pointing.

When he finally saw that the coast was clear, he turned around and pulled off his ski mask with a sigh. He had only worn it in case of a situation like he had just dealt with. It was against Guild policy to approach targets with your face obscured. Tripper cautiously craned his neck around the corner and looked at the room. It was still closed. He stuffed the ski mask in a cargo pocket on his pants and made his way back over to the target door.

Tripper pressed his ear to the door, but he couldn't hear anything. He stepped back away from it and unlocked it with a universal key card that he swiped from the front desk when he came back from the diner. With a quick buzz and a click, the door gently swung open. Both beds were empty. A shotgun was racked behind the door. Tripper slammed against the door with all his might and came to a sudden stop when he heard a man grunt and the shotgun fall to the floor. He jumped back from the door and fired one round into it about chest high. There was a great crash as a very short, very fat bald man fell onto the bed. Tripper listened to the man grunt as he pulled himself up onto the bed closest the door.

"Mayhew, you rat fuck," gurgled the man. "I should have put a hit on you back in Muncie, you Guild rat fuck."

"It's an extreme displeasure to see you as well, Rourke," responded Tripper, flatly. "Where's the file?"

Francis Rourke had finally managed to pull himself up onto the bed. His breathing was heavy, and he was sweating profusely, but Tripper saw no blood or wounds. If he really was having this much trouble, it had nothing to do with being shot. "Fuck you, Mayhew. That's where it is."

Tripper tracked Rourke with his weapon as he sat up on the other side of the bed and looked over his shoulder at the door. Rourke took a moment to wipe his brow with the palm of his hand and inspect his sweat like a foreign substance. He looked down at his shirt and dropped his shoulders. "Look at this. You ruined my favorite god damn shirt. You Commie rat fuck."

Tripper looked at the wrinkles set in the shirt from where Rourke had been sleeping in it. "Where's the file, Rourke?"

All at once Rourke stood up, reached into the nightstand and pulled out a .38 snub nose. Tripper jumped out of the door way and pressed himself up against the wall. Rourke fired twice and missed both times. Tripper fired one shot and grazed Rourke's left shoulder. Rourke dropped the gun and let out a Wilhelm-like scream. He clutched his shoulder and fell to his knees. Tripper calmly walked over toward Rourke and holstered his weapon. He waited until Rourke looked up at him before he hit him across the face with a back handed slap at about fifty percent power. He only gave Rourke a moment to react before doing the same with the other hand. Rourke sat on his knees breathing heavy.

Tripper looked down and saw that the palm of the black nitralon glove on his right hand had been torn open. He ripped off his broken glove and pulled another one out of his back pocket. "I don't like you, Rourke. I don't like you; I don't like what you do. I don't like your laissez-faire attitude toward dumping bio-hazardous waste into city water supplies. Or your brilliant idea of switching fluoride with ethylene glycol to save on spending. I hate your trophy skank wife and your child molesting faggot son." Tripper snapped on the replacement glove, pulled his gun out of its holster and hit Rourke in the face with it. Rourke's head snapped to the side with Tripper's punch. Tripper's rage simmered without losing steam. "With that being said, I'm not gonna kill you if I don't fucking have to." Tripper pressed the barrel of his gun to Rourke's head until the skin indented and turned red. "Now you can either tell me where the contract is, or I will force you to lose your safety deposit," Tripper cocked the Glock with one thumb, "and I'll find it anyway."

Rourke looked up at Tripper with an evil Kubrick stare, mucus dripping out of his nose, his teeth blood stained. There was a quick sharp *zip* sound near the door before Tripper flew backwards clutching his throat with his free hand. Candace Rourke pulled back on the garroting wire with all her might. She craned her neck around Tripper's head and smiled at him with a look of insanity he had only seen on wax figures. He marched backwards trying to take the crushing pressure off his throat and slam Candace into the wall or the TV. In a few quick steps, he aimed his gun at Rourke and fired three shots. Candace slammed into the open door, driving the door knob into the back, which stopped her only briefly. He heard her gasp as the doorknob slammed into her kidneys, then she tightened her hold on the wire.

She pressed her mouth to Tripper's ear and he could feel her hot stale breath on his skin as she whispered, "Still think I'm a miserable fucking whore?"

At this, Tripper slammed the elbow of his free arm into her stomach, then stepped on Candace's foot on the opposite side. Candace let out a primal animal-like scream and her grip on the wire loosened. Tripper worked his fingers under the wire and ripped it away from his throat. He spun around and punched Candace in the side of the head with his free hand, sending her out of the room and landing face first on the ground eight feet away from the pool. Tripper coughed violently trying to get used to breathing again. After a few moments, he looked out the hotel room door and saw Candace crawling across the stiff green indoor-outdoor carpet towards the pool. The high heel of the corresponding foot that Tripper had stomped on was broken. The heel laid on the transom as Candace drug the rest of the shoe along, dangling uselessly off her foot. Still standing in the room, Tripper aimed at the back of her head and fired twice before flying into another coughing jag. He spoke to her lifeless body once he could breathe again.

"And...my direct words...were trophy skank wife." He put his hands on both knees and coughed again.

Just then, a tremendous force hit him from behind, knocking him out of the room and into the indoor courtyard. The inertia of the hit rushed him towards the body of Candace Rourke, which he promptly tripped over and fell to the ground. The tremendous force rolled over top of him, pressing Tripper's flailing body into Candace's lifeless one before creating an equally tremendous splash in the pool. Tripper felt a thick vise like grip tighten around his ankle as he began sliding backwards. His eyes widened in panic and he quickly began grasping at anything he thought might slow him down. He grabbed onto Candace's outstretched lifeless arms and squeezed her wrists as tightly as he could. The world came into sharp, supernatural clarity as Tripper watched Candace's body begin to slide toward him at the same rate of speed that he was sliding into the pool. The stiff plastic carpet and the hotel room door all slipped from view as he disappeared under the water in seconds.

Under the water, Tripper kicked both legs furiously as he tried to swim toward the surface, but he sank rapidly to the bottom as only one leg would move. He heard a loud splash above him. He couldn't feel his left leg and brain's initial thought was that he couldn't swim because his leg had, in fact, been bitten off by a shark. Tripper looked down just in time to see Rourke let go of his ankle and begin to climb up his body like a ladder; his evil smile still intact, bloody teeth and all. Tripper reached behind his back and pulled a six-inch tactical knife out of its sheath. With everything he had he slammed it into the side of Rourke's neck and then gave it a quarter turn. Cloudy red blood began to pour out of the wound. Tripper tried once again to swim upwards, but he stopped suddenly as if he had hit a ceiling. Candace's lifeless hand floated in front of his face in a cloud of bubbles. Tripper brushed it aside and reached above his head to guide her body away from him and then made his way to the surface in three strong kicks and no oxygen.

He broke the surface of the pool with a long deep gasp for air, before bobbing back down under the water. When he came back up again, he reached his arms out in front of himself and flailed blindly until he felt the concrete of the pool edge. With a great amount of effort, he pulled himself and sixty pounds of wet clothes up onto dry ground. His eyes and nose burned from the chlorine and his lungs were on fire, but he hadn't felt that alive in a long time. He laid his face against the ground and looked down the length of the pool toward the row of rooms on the first floor beneath his. He closed his eyes and took a few deep raspy breaths.

"Need some help up?" came a familiar voice from somewhere over top of him.

Tripper opened his eyes and saw a pair of black leather combat boots inches in front of his face. "Montana London, I presume?" he turned his face toward the ground and coughed out a mouthful of water.

Tripper watched from the corner of his eye as the black-clad legs knelt down and Montana held out her sickly pale hand. He looked back toward the ground, set down his gun and gave her the finger. She straightened up again and stood motionless next to him. Tripper coughed once more, then he slowly began to make his way to his knees, then his feet.

"So, how ya been?" he said sarcastically.

"You had the building evacuated and locked all of the exits, Tripper," Montana said matter-of-factly. "It took a minute to get in."

Tripper stood and began to leisurely wipe off a few of Candace's stray hairs that had stuck to his hands. "Really? Four, five years? Took you that long did it?" He turned toward Montana and looked her square in the eye. Montana stared back at him. He hadn't been stared down by her in a long time, but it didn't have the effect on him that it used to. Without a word, she lifted a manila envelope and handed it to Tripper. Tripper gazed at her for a second before ripping it out of her hand. He glared coldly into her face and opened the envelope then looked inside. He flipped through a couple of papers then closed it again. After setting his jaw, he walked straight past Montana, hitting her shoulder with his.

When Montana reached Tripper's hotel room, he was already half naked and ripping clean clothes out of his duffel bag and talking on his phone in German. He stopped momentarily when he saw her in the doorway then continued to get dressed and hung up his phone.

"You can take a shower if you want," she said calmly.

"No, Ms. London, I can't," Tripper called from the bathroom. "I have less than enough time to get changed out of soaking wet clothes and into new before the fucking cops get here, so I can drive all night to the fucking field office in Frankenmuth."

Montana slowly looked around the room taking in every detail. She could still see the ghosts of where he set up his equipment and cleaned his gun. He kept a good room. And he cleaned it up well. She cautiously sat down on the edge of the bed and called to Tripper in the bathroom. "The cops aren't coming."

Tripper rattled around in the bathroom then stuck his head out of the door. "What?"

"I intercepted the call from the Ramada Inn. Nobody's coming. You don't have to travel covered in chlorine."

Tripper thought about it for a moment then ducked back into the bathroom. He knew she wasn't lying. Montana didn't have a sense of humor like that. But he knew that there had to be an angle.

Montana sat on the edge of the bed listening to the sounds in the bathroom, her eyes wide in the dark and fang flashing smirk. Finally, after an unnecessarily long pause, Tripper turned on the shower.

Montana tightened her lips and nodded her head at the sound. After only a handful of minutes, Tripper shut off the water and stepped out the bathroom fully clothed and drying his hair. Montana had not moved from her spot on the bed.

Tripper glanced over at her then pulled a pair of socks out his duffel bag and sat in a chair on the opposite side of the room. He stared at Montana, waiting for her to say something. Montana sat motionless, her wild hair silhouetted by the light coming through the window from the courtyard. She stared at Tripper from the corner of her eye, her eyebrows raised, waiting for him to speak. When Tripper finally put on his shoes, he stopped moving altogether.

"Well?" he said with a shrug.

"How ya been?" Montana spoke as if that was the first time she had ever said the phrase.

"That's it? A quick *how ya been* and then you book town?"

"Not quite." Her voice was very low, and her words carefully spoken.

"What then?" he said shrugging again.

"I understand that you are upset with me. And I also understand why, but you do not know the reasons for my actions and I, therefore, think that your anger is justified where your resentment is not."

Tripper wiped the bridge of his nose with his thumb, "Ok. Care to explain?"

Montana stared at the strange pattern on the carpet. "I will." With all the sharpness of a bullwhip her eyes shot up and looked Tripper straight in his. "But not right now. We have to go."

"We?"

"Yes."

"And by *we* you mean *you*, right? Because, I think somebody may have already told you, I have to be in Frankenmuth before dawn and I haven't slept."

"I know you think I abandoned you, Trip. And I haven't given you reason to think otherwise, but you haven't been alone these last five years. I've known where you are and what you've been doing on all your assignments. That message, from the waitress at the diner?"

"Cammy."

"Yeah. That was from me."

"Oh. So, you'll talk to your other recruits, but you won't talk to me."

"Why the hell would İ recruit a waitress?"

Tripper was stopped dead. The stone-cold logic of that statement started to put everything else into focus. The message did have a Montana-esque ring to it now that he thought about it. He felt his muscles slowly relax when he didn't even know they were tense to start with.

"I just knew you'd sooner take a message from her than from me."

"Ok," he said quietly.

"I need your help, Tripper. I've been assigned to something that is too big for me to go in alone."

"Have you talked to the Home Office?"

"Yes. And they approved. I was given this assignment about twenty-four hours ago. It's time sensitive and needs to be carried out on the fourth."

Tripper pulled out his phone and looked at the date. He should have been able to rattle it off, but his brain was fuzzy. "It's the thirty fir--- it's the first. We have three days. Where is it?"

"Los Angeles."

"Do we have flight coupons?"

"I do. You don't. So, we will have to drive."

"Christ. How long will that take?"

"About thirty-six hours. If we don't stop and we both drive."

"When do you want to start?"

"Now."

CHAPTER FOURTEEN

Snake Eyes

Tripper dropped his duffel bag on top of the hard-plastic equipment case in the trunk next to Montana's gear. When he opened the passenger door of the shiny new Buick Lacrosse, Montana leaned over from the driver's seat and looked up at him.

"Ready?" she asked, more out of courtesy than genuine interest.

"Yeah," Tripper sat down in the seat.

In his mind, he instantly flashed back to his car ride with Montana from Fallingwater five years earlier. He began to hum *Over the Electric Grapevine* to himself but was stopped when Montana started the engine. *Goodness Gracious* by Ellie Goulding screamed and chirped over the sound system. Tripper flew backwards in his seat then grabbed a hold of the dashboard. Montana stomped her foot on the gas and the car shot out of the Days Inn parking lot and onto North Canal Road before turning onto the West Saginaw Highway.

The car flew through the dark, Montana and Tripper sitting in silence, the radio blaring away until the album ended. When it stopped, Montana pushed the power button on the radio without looking at it, gripping the wheel with all the intensity of a pilot docking a ship on a star destroyer. Tripper looked over at the wheel and could tell even by the dim lights of the dash that the skin over the knuckles of her pale hands was white.

"Y' alright?" he asked cautiously, raising both eyebrows. "You're grippin' it kinda tight there."

"It's a little after three," she said glancing at the dash clock, "if I'm lucky I can get to Long Beach before dawn."

"You got a propulsion system in this thing I don't know about?"

"Long Beach, Indiana," she said coldly.

"Gotcha," said Tripper, turning to look out his window. They said nothing for a few minutes until they came up on a sign declaring future exits. "Hey, we're gonna be passing through Battle Creek," he said with cynical excitement.

"Hungry?" Montana asked, reaching for the temperature dial.

"No, I was thinking more about the Daisy Zick case. She was a victim of an unsolved homicide in 1963."

"Yeah, I know, I wrote a paper on it in high school," Montana was starting to loosen up a little bit.

"Was that for...home-ec?" Tripper said, trying to be funny.

"Sex ed," she stated flatly.

Tripper smiled to himself. "You know, I think that was the first time I've heard you make a joke."

"I'm sorry, I won't do it anymore."

"That's not what I meant."

"That was another joke," she slowly turned her head toward Tripper, her eyes cutting through the darkness of the cab into his, "Ha-ha," she said with an almost mocking mechanical delivery. She stared at him for a moment then turned back toward the road and glanced at the clock. "I don't think we're gonna make it there before dawn. Can you check for me, please?"

Tripper took out his phone and pulled up a map application, "Long Beach, right?"

"Yes."

Tripper flipped through his phone for a minute before Montana spoke again. "If we are going to do this together, we will have to get some things out on the table before we get there," she said in her business-like tone.

"Alright," Tripper said with a sigh as he looked up from the map on his phone.

"You are sexually attracted to me," she spoke without any sort of emotion.

Tripper side-eyed her with the expression of someone who has just heard a person's deepest and darkest secret. He sat in stunned silence for an uncomfortable amount of time. "When you put it like that you make me sound like a serial rapist," he replied with a mixture of pained anger and fear of what she was going to say next.

"It doesn't bother me," she said in the same emotionless way.

Tripper kept his eyes locked on her, but faced her only slightly. He nodded and responded in a confused sarcastic tone. "I'm glad we got that cleared up."

"I've met guys who wanted to fuck me, but you seem more interested in me than that."

"Okay."

"Why?"

"Why am I interested or why do they want to fuck you?"

"They want to fuck me because I'm a sideshow to them. I don't know why you are interested at all. You are far too intelligent to like me."

"I can safely say that that makes no sense whatsoever."

"You're smart, Tripper. The guys who like me aren't. So, what about me are you attracted to? This is something I've never understood about you and I have pondered for quite some time."

Tripper blinked tightly then opened his eyes wide, running his palm across his forehead into his hair. His left eye started to twitch. "Well, that is...something that would be very difficult to explain."

"Is it because you think I am a *freak*?" she asked in her same flat manner.

"Jesus Fuck, no!" Tripper wiped his face with both hands and tilted his head back.

Montana showed the slightest expression of confusion at Tripper's reaction. She kept her eyes on the road and continued to drive.

"Look," Tripper finally said, exasperated. "I like you, alright? You know it. I know it. That's out on the table. I don't think of you as a sideshow or a freak show or anything like that that anyone has said about you. You've got this...cold, unfeeling robot arm approach to how you talk to people sometimes that isn't really conducive to sensitive conversation---"

"I feel a lot of things. I just don't broadcast it like a god damn satellite dish."

"Good to know," Tripper said with a slow deep nod. For some reason he found Montana's use of profanity comforting, which gave him a handle to grab onto and help himself slow down. "I understand your desire, your need to address something like this before going into a job with someone, but this is a much larger conversation that I personally can't get into when I'm preparing to commit burglary."

"I understand that," Montana nodded in solidarity. The two had managed to meet on solid ground from separate sides of a playing field. "I want you to know that I am a-sexual, and I don't feel about you the way you feel about me. But it doesn't bother me that you do."

"O-kay," Tripper said slowly. He could feel their conversational boat drift rapidly from shore.

"You're the first person that has been sexually attracted to me that truly likes *me*, though I do not know why. I'm awkward, some say stand-offish, I'm ugly and I don't get along with people. You're a good co-worker, Tripper, and a decent person and I would very much like to be your friend, but I can't be anything more than that to you and I don't want you to get upset about that. This is new territory for me."

"I find your openness both refreshing and encouraging, Montana. I'm sorry I've caused you any sort of consternation. But you have a really weird way of showing people that you want to be friends."

"I didn't know how to tell you in email and I didn't want to upset you. I've also been very busy."

Tripper nodded and chewed his bottom lip, his eyes zoned out on the dashboard. They sat in silence for a few miles before he spoke again. "You have very nice hair," he said in a matter of fact way of his own.

"I have the worst kept hair in the history of the western hemisphere, Tripper."

Tripper shrugged slightly, "Well…"

"Not even guys that have wanted to fuck me liked my hair."

"Like you said, they're stupid."

"Maybe you're just strange."

"It's been said before."

Montana paused for a moment before she spoke. "Would you like to touch my hair?" she said calmly.

Tripper both raised and furrowed his brow in confusion. "What?"

"I'm not one to touch or be touched but I will let you touch my hair. If you would like to do so."

Tripper looked around the car as if the correct response was written somewhere on the upholstery. "Is this going to bother you while you drive?"

"If you pull it or do something stupid, yeah. In which case, I will kick you out of the car and drive back to unload several firearms into your face." She let that hang a moment before adding, "That was a joke."

Tripper was now a little bit afraid, but he didn't show it.

Montana sighed and glanced down at the display on the radio. "This is a lot of build up about nothing. You're going to be disappointed."

Tripper moved to raise his hand. Montana sat very still and looked straight ahead. With all the care one would use to touch a Faberge egg, Tripper touched the back of Montana's head. Her hair felt both soft and wiry. Something inside of Tripper was suddenly very calm. He ran his fingers through her hair a couple of times before taking his hand away. Montana showed no reaction.

"Disappointed?" she asked in an almost militaristic fashion.

"Not at all," he said, trying to imitate her emotionless delivery. "Your hair is great. Never touch it."

CHAPTER FIFTEEN

Homework

They hit Vegas with about four hours left in their trip. The drive had been held in near complete silence, except for the radio. During Tripper's first turn at the wheel he learned to leave the music choices up to Montana. He had hooked up his phone and turned on White Zombie's *La Sexorcisto* only to be met with Montana's no-nonsense glare from the corner of her eye as she tried to sleep. He flipped through a couple of different bands and genres and still wound up on the receiving end of those same slits of ice blue. Finally, he just gave up and hummed to himself and played the album in his head. Several times he tried to start conversations with Montana, who always gave dismissive and unenthusiastic answers, eventually leading Tripper to give that up too. But as they approached Las Vegas on I-15 Tripper decided to press his luck one more time.

"Montana?" Tripper glanced in the rearview in an effort to look busy.

"Mm-hmm." Montana was curled up in the passenger seat facing the window, her jacket draped over her like a blanket.

"I never really got a chance, well, I avoided the subject really, then I was dragged screaming out of your hotel room but...you did know about Shady Acres, right? Back at LMJ?"

"Yeah, what about it?" her face was pressed against the seat, distorting her pronunciation.

"Did you ever go there?"

"No. Did you?"

"Yeah."

"And? What'd you think?" Her reply was sarcastic, as if Tripper was trying to discuss the apartments he had looked at before starting college.

"There was *a lot* fucked up about that place, like...*Donnie Velvet* fucked up."

"Mm-hmm." Montana had no idea what Tripper was talking about, so she decided to wait for context clues.

"But," he took one hand off the wheel and ran it through his hair. The memory was burned into his brain, but it was the first time he had ever relayed the experience to someone else. "the one bedroom was converted into, like, a server room. There was a big server and a computer and three monitors on this desk in the corner. And all the monitors had live video feeds on them. Most of the feeds were rooms in the house, but one was of some hotel room *here*."

Montana opened one eye and looked out her window just in time to see the reinforcement wall of a freeway exit ramp, then closed it again. "Define *here*."

Tripper turned to his left as they passed Treasure Island about three hundred yards away. "Vegas." His voice was incredulous as he looked over at Montana and then her view out the window.

"Ok. And?"

"Do you know what the hell?"

Montana gave up on the prospect of sleep and sat up in her seat. She brushed her hair out of her face and then itched her nose with both hands. "Well, based on what you are saying, I'm assuming that you went into a completed house?"

"Yes," Tripper was reminded of his conspiracy theory conversations with Penn and adjusted in his seat, leaning in toward the wheel. "They finished two houses before, or in spite of, the development being scrapped. I went in one of them."

Montana had taken a drink of water as Tripper was talking and was delayed in her response as she swallowed. She put the cap back on the bottle and started speaking. "Now's as good a time as any, I guess. Most of the employees at ISE and Crystal Communications, well the higher ups at least, are pretty sick fucks as I imagine you've already gathered."

"Yeah."

"Every year, the top dogs at ISE and Crystal Comm get together for a little soiree on the Fourth of July. You've been to one."

"Fallingwater."

"Yes. Those parties are always held at a building designed by Frank Lloyd Wright that they have stolen from us. Wright was one of the earliest Guild members and, so far, most famous and prolific, although only other Guild members are aware of who and what he was. Sadly, many of the Wright properties have been stolen from us over the years, barring the temporary structures and few that were destroyed before his death. But we are trying to get them back."

"Aren't most of them privately owned?"

"A good portion of them. By Guild members. The remaining buildings are owned by small firms and companies that are Guild associated."

"I don't get it."

"What?" Montana snapped her head toward Tripper.

"Why Wright? I mean, I get that he was a member and everything, but why his buildings? What's so important?"

"They're more symbolic than anything else, I suppose." Montana slowly turned back toward the windshield. "Art, math, science, engineering, architecture, history, freedom of expression, creative thought. Pushing the boundaries and trying to elevate a given craft. These are all tenants of the Guild's philosophy. They're the very foundation of what we believe in. It's what we are fighting so hard to protect. And every time one of those greasy fucks takes one away from us, they're spitting in the face of that."

Tripper continued to run his hand through his hair as he listened to Montana. Something about driving, the hum of the road and the pattern of her speech was very Zen. "How many Wright buildings are there?"

"In America? Three hundred and seventy-eight. Still standing."

"Jesus," Tripper bit his bottom lip and squinted his eyes. There weren't that many Guild members. "How do they know where it's going to happen?"

"They used the Oscars to communicate to each other." There was a low buzz of resentment in Montana's voice.

"What, like a code?"

"Of a sort. The Genius Bars at ISE thought that they were clever and assigned each Best Picture nomination to a specific Wright building. Back in 2017, Hell or High Water was the Kalita Humphrey's Theater in Dallas, Manchester by the Sea was the Theodore Baird House in Massachusetts, Arrival was the Como Orchard Summer Colony in the *state* of Montana," she rolled her eyes toward Tripper and held them there for a moment then looked back out the front window, "Hidden Figures was the Andrew B. Cooke House in Virginia, Hacksaw Ridge was the Luis Marsden House, also in Virginia."

"Clever."

"Not exactly the Funkschlüssel C, but we give them points for trying."

"What about that other one?"

"Which one? The foreign film?"

"Yeah, that one."

"Lion was a wildcard. In the case of a wildcard, we would have stationed a Guild member at every lost property we could and hoped to get lucky. But, as you remember, that didn't happen that year."

"No, the cards got screwed up."

"They figured out that we knew." Montana's voice was frosty and unwelcoming. She examined her fingernails as she spoke.

"The Guild has been around since, what, World War II and it took them that long to figure out that we were hip to the scheme?"

"They didn't start doing it until the '70's really. After that they stole enough properties from us that they could start playing their stupid little games."

"But wait, Moonlight won that year."

"But first it was La La Land," Montana raised one eyebrow and cocked her head toward Tripper, still staring at her fingernails.

"What buildings were they for?"

"Florida Southern College and Hollyhock House in Los Angeles."

"But it wound up at Fallingwater."

"Code name: Fences."

"And Hollyhock is where we are going now? What was the code name this year?"

"Oh, they don't use that anymore. The switch at the 89TH was their last sort of *fuck you* to the Guild."

"What do they do now?"

"The Emmys."

"Of course."

"But the pattern really doesn't make sense, so I suspect it's a rouse."

Tripper sat quietly for a quarter mile or so, mulling everything over. In the several years that he had been in the Guild, he had learned to receive and digest large quantities of information quickly, but he still liked to take his time when he could. "How does it connect to Shady Acres?"

"Shady Acres was a sort of annex. A year-round vacation bungalow for smaller get-togethers. The video feed, to which you were earlier referring, was transmitting to a penthouse suite at the Magic Carpet Hotel and Casino in downtown Las Vegas; their base of operations." Once Montana finished speaking she stared out the window looking up at a passing airplane. All this information was so old hat to her she could recite it in her sleep.

Tripper gave an expression like his brain hurt. "Why?"

"Why would middle aged men want to watch a live feed of a sex dungeon torture chamber?" Montana turned to Tripper and said rather plainly, "What you should be asking is how many more Shady Acres are there in the country."

Tripper tapped his mouth with the back of his index finger, "How many?"

Montana held her gaze on Tripper for an uncomfortably long amount of time, until he turned toward her and met her eyes. For the first time, Tripper was able to read her. Her cold intense stares actually contained messages. Secret messages that only people who knew her could see.

Montana set her jaw and turned back to the road.

* * *

Los Angeles didn't notice when they came in. Montana drove through Glendale, down the Golden State Freeway to Los Feliz. Tripper watched the sonic-magenta sun slowly dip behind the dingy gold landscape of urban California and his mind shot back to *Blade Runner*. When they stopped at the intersection of Observation Avenue, a guy a little bit younger than Tripper stepped out into the crosswalk just in time for a Lexus to blow the red light and race past him, clipping his pelvis with its side mirror, sending him to the

THE FIVE YEAR TRIP   -   191

ground screaming through his teeth in pain as broken mirror and fiberglass showered down on top of him. A woman on a cell phone watched the whole thing and crossed the street, passing the screaming sweating man with little more than a downward glance. The town looked nothing like the Los Angeles of the future, but the attitude was right.

The Buick lolled through the slalom up Deronda Drive to a small single level ranch house. The house was made of dark brick and stucco with small clusters of hyacinth blooming in the woodchip filled planters that ran alongside the walkway. Montana got out of the car without saying a word, leaving Tripper to unbuckle and catch up with her on the path to the door. She lifted a small stone sculpture of a sleeping deer no bigger than a garden gnome that sat next to the door and pulled a copper colored house key out of a compartment recessed in its base. Tripper looked around at the neighborhood. It reminded him very much of some of the higher-class neighborhoods back east, but with smog, on a scrubby rather than tree-lined hill and the Los Angeles skyline in the background.

Montana opened the door setting off the alarm. She very coolly walked over to the panel on the wall and punched in a series of numbers shutting it off.

"Is this your place?" Tripper looked around.

Montana's eyes flashed at his as she held her finger to her lips and shook her head. One of Tripper's cold waves came to visit him again. Montana reached under her jacket and pulled out her Glock as she began to slowly move through the house. Tripper snapped himself out of it quick enough to pull his weapon and creep along behind her. Montana glanced over her shoulder and motioned for Tripper to go in the opposite way. He stopped for a second then switched directions.

It was an expensive house, but modestly furnished and decorated. Lots of dark wood and furniture of deep velvety greys and chocolate browns. Tripper made his way into a den with a large, dark, hickory desk and tall backed dark leather chair. The wood paneled walls sported a few degrees, which he didn't bother to read, and a few Grant Wood paintings that looked like originals, but he didn't bother to check. He crept around the desk and found a small black steel safe burrowed into the wall behind the desk. The keypad numbers and display screen glowed soft lime green in the dimly lit den.

"We good?"

Montana's voice in the doorway sent Tripper an inch and a half into the air, but fast enough that no one saw it.

"Yep, good." Tripper casually collected himself and re-holstered his weapon.

"Let's get the bags before we head out again."

"Whose house are we in exactly?"

"He's another Guild member. I asked him if we could stay here a few nights while we did a job."

Tripper bristled at Montana talking casually about another guy. He bit the back of his tongue and spoke without attitude. "Is this a common practice?"

Montana walked about a step and half in front of Tripper to the car. She added the house key to her ring and popped the trunk with the car key. "Age old tradition," she spoke in her classic tone of sarcasm. Tripper felt good not being on the receiving end of it. "The argument could be made that we invented the Air BnB, but mostly we just refer to it as couch surfing. It comes in handy when there are no Guild-friendly hotels in the area or you get a job on short notice."

"So where is Mr. Darkwood, anyway?" Tripper dropped his duffel bag and equipment case on floor to the entry way.

Montana gestured with her head to the back of the house where she had investigated earlier. "Galveston. And drop the tone."

The décor in Tripper's room was identical to the décor in the den and the rest of the house. He checked the Wood painting hanging on the wall opposite his bed. Original. The large window the size of a decent sized flat screen stuffed into the wall over his dark grey bed overlooked the twinkling Los Angeles skyline to the south east.

"It's a decent neighborhood, if you're worried about that sort of thing," Montana called from somewhere in the house but nearby. "It's no different than your average UMC suburban utopia." She managed to maintain her sarcastic inflection even while shouting.

* * *

"If the world-famous Hollywood Boulevard was on the east coast it would be known locally as a strip mall," Tripper thought to himself after they rolled through the night, past a print shop, a pizzeria and a taco stand.

Montana sucked on a fang with her tongue and waited for the light to turn. Tripper pulled a pack of peanut M&Ms out of an inside jacket pocket. He tore it open and popped a few into his mouth to prove to Montana that they weren't poisoned before he offered her the bag.

"Where is Santa Monica Boulevard from here?" he asked, sounding the most like a tourist he ever had in his life.

Montana looked disdainfully out of the corner of her eyes at the bag of M&Ms and gave a small quick shake of her head. "South. Why?"

"Do you think we could pass by there on the way back?" he slammed a fistful of M&Ms into his mouth.

Montana turned her head toward Tripper with Nosferatu-like speed and intensity. "Why?"

Tripper stared out the window at the traffic light and shrugged. "I always wanted to see where The Doors recorded LA Woman."

Montana creaked her head back toward the steering wheel and dropped it into her hand.

"Light's green," Tripper said with a mouthful.

Montana stepped on the gas, her head still lowered into her palm. She drove a few feet before lifting her eyes to the road and driving with one hand as she held her head in the other.

"Are you sure you don't want an M&M?" Tripper held the bag out to her.

"I'm allergic to peanuts," she said, monotone.

"Yeah," Tripper chuckled. "You can't do gluten, either. Am I going to see you eating a peanut butter sandwich later, too?"

Montana dropped her head into her hand again and rubbed her eyes, "*What?*"

"Back at LMJ, Hunter offered you a donut and you said you couldn't do gluten. Later I watched you eat a sandwich and a granola bar."

Montana stared out the windshield with her deadpan look. Tripper looked at her with eyebrows raised. "Do you really have an allergy, or do you just not want any?"

Montana waited for a while before she answered. "I don't like the ones with peanuts."

Tripper began rooting around in his pockets, "I think I have a different bag in here."

Montana flipped on her turn signal and directed the car toward a driveway that ran alongside yet another scrubby hill up to Barnsdall Art Park. "We're here."

Tripper looked out his window and finished chewing as he stuffed the bag back into his jacket pocket. "This is Hollyhock, huh?"

"The driveway to it, at least."

A large white utility van made the curve in the driveway about seventy-five yards away. Tripper caught a flash of the Green Room Catering logo on its side.

"There's a blast from the past," he said low.

Montana glanced over at him then did a double take. "What are you doing?"

"What?" Tripper was becoming concerned.

"Keep chewing and stop looking so scared." She turned back toward the road and made a face that on anyone else would have projected the illusion of being deep in thought. On Montana, it looked cartoonish and over the top. Clearly, she had seen people make the face before, but she could not convincingly make it herself. Tripper wondered if she had ever applied that much tension to her facial muscles or used them in that configuration before.

They passed the catering van with no incident. The driver didn't appear to be all that interested in life, let alone the two people in the dark sedan cruising up the hill. The bizarre expression on Montana's face slowly fell as they reached the top. Tripper became very self-conscious about the volume of his chewing.

"How much do you know about this?"

"The house or the event?"

"Both."

"The house: enough. The event," Montana pulled into a spot in the deserted parking lot near a set of stairs leading up to the house, "little."

The sound of the engine died down and the car became silent except for Montana shifting in her seat as she unbuckled. The chirping of crickets and sporadic screams of nighttime echoed up from the street. Tripper squinted his eyes. Montana placed her hand on her door opener and then snapped her head toward him.

"What?"

"Do you hear it?" Tripper kept his eyes squinted and turned toward Montana.

"What?" Her inflection and delivery were the same.

"Music. But it's close."

They opened their doors in unison and leaned their heads out to listen. Montana's eyes shot up to the house as Tripper stepped out of the car.

"What is it?"

Tripper walked around to the rear of the car and looked up and down the property as far as he could see. "It's familiar, but I can't place it. It's distorted. Like bad speakers."

The music stopped. Montana looked up at Tripper and he glanced over his shoulder back at her. She stepped out of the car and walked over to Tripper, silently locking the car with the remote key.

"Where was it coming from?"

Tripper shook his head, signaling Montana to stop talking. They stood silently for a moment before he gestured to the house. As if on cue, the music started again. A low ominous Spanish inspired guitar riff rolled out of the dark and echoed forebodingly through the walls and trees of Hollyhock. They looked at each other and Tripper raised his eyebrows with a slight grin.

"What is it?" Montana whispered.

Tripper hummed along. "God damn it," he whispered.

Montana took off for the stairs with Tripper in tow. They moved east down the sidewalk toward the Los Angeles Municipal Art Gallery. The scuffing and scraping of their boots on the cement traveled through the night like auditory emergency flares. Every time they moved, Tripper felt like they were giving away their position to some unseen enemy. He hoped that the military drum cadence of the music would cover up their footsteps.

Tripper's eyes widened, and he jumped ahead a few paces to tap Montana on the shoulder. "It's White Rabbit!" he whispered hoarsely.

Grace Slick's voice buzzed through some sort of outdoor sound system and chased itself and the rest of the music in a circle around the building.

Montana instantly slowed almost to a dead stop. "What?" In the blackness of night, the dark circles around her eyes cast her ice blue into a deep dark abyss. The music cut out long enough for Montana's whispered "What?" to sound like a scream in the night, then pop back on, more steady and clear than before.

"Jefferson Airplane. White Rabbit." Tripper pointed in the darkness to where it sounded like there was a speaker near the roof of the art gallery.

Montana held her fist to her mouth rubbing her two front teeth with the knuckle of her thumb as she looked at the ground somewhere diagonally behind Tripper. She stood there like that for a moment, her eyes distant and deep in thought. Finally, she turned around and walked back in the direction they had came. The song spoke of men on chessboards as Tripper followed Montana down the sidewalk through a dense, manmade forest of pine trees to the front of the building. A large art deco concrete over hang broke the pattern of evenly spaced conifers like a set piece from a late 60s sci fi film. Montana stopped before the overhang and reached into her pocket then turned to Tripper.

"Do you have a flashlight on you?"

Tripper thought there was something odd about the building. Montana's question made him realize that there were no lights on anywhere on the property. Any light that they had to see by was emitted from random sources in the distance. He reached into his pocket and pulled out his phone, clicking on the light. Montana's cold fingers politely took the phone from Tripper's hand and directed the phone toward the art gallery's entrance.

"And this year's homecoming theme is..." Montana imitated an overly excited cheerleader.

The beam sliced through the dark with all the delicacy of a cake cutter. Cool blue LED rolled over the cement sidewalk to the glass doors then dropped and froze. A black and white chessboard sat square to the building on a crooked dirty doormat. In the center of the board was a single red chess piece; a queen. The entire cabin crew of United Flight Jefferson Airplane reminded Montana and Tripper about what a Dormouse said one time.

The music faded out and was silent for a moment before it started playing over again. Tripper stood leaning on his knees with his hands looking at the ambitious and avant-garde diorama on the porch of the Los Angeles Municipal Art Gallery. He stood up and looked over at Montana who stood blank faced and obscured behind the glow of the phone's flashlight.

"Kinda on the *nose*, don' 'cha think? At least they got their sound system working."

Montana adjusted her grip on the phone and clicked off the flashlight, handing it back to Tripper. "They're assholes."

* * *

Tripper slept restlessly, tossing and turning the whole night, waking up from obscure dreams about clocks, old jobs, and menacing unseen threats. At one point in the night he dreamt of being lost in a surrealistic Midwest landscape, surrounded by large round knobby hills and being chased by a Jolly Green Giant sized white rabbit with a Volkswagen sized pocket watch and bleeding prominent front teeth. Montana sat on a far-off hill in a big floppy hat, dressed like Scarlett O'Hara, eating petit fours. After a chase of what felt like miles, he came to staring at the Grant Wood painting hanging on the wall opposite the bed. He cursed Mr. Darkwood for his warm and comforting interior design choices then rolled over toward the wall.

Somewhere around five or six in the morning he gave up trying to sleep. He ventured out into the living room and the kitchen beyond. The distinctive sound of a gun being cleaned rolled out from under Montana's bedroom door. For the rest of the day after that, he heard the muffled sounds of panting and grunting followed by periods of rest. He didn't see her until somewhere around four that afternoon.

Montana stepped out of her room fully dressed in her gear, tying back her wild jet-black hair with a matching scrunchy. She walked into the kitchen and took a bottle of water out of the fridge. Tripper was laying on a brown leather couch in the living room, re-reading *Chaos* by Tim O'Neill.

"You didn't have to stay in there all day, you know."

Even though Montana was behind him, he could still feel the look she shot him.

"I once spent several months using a broom closet as an office. It's no fun."

Montana walked into the living room and stood over top of Tripper. Her presence in the living room was commanding and her intensity was as unsettling as it always was, but Tripper wasn't going to give it to her.

"Are you ready?"

Tripper took his time finishing a sentence, then dropped the book on his chest and looked up at Montana with a pleasant smile. Her normally off-putting glare was suddenly very comical. Tripper stretched out his arms and curled his feet inside of his socks.

"Hey there, you! I was just doing some research, brushing up on some history. Hey, I like what you did with your hair."

Montana was not amused. Tripper let the tension hang there for a moment, waiting to see who would break first. He did.

"You ready to go?" His smile to her still went un-reciprocated. "Let me get dressed, I'll take you out. Take you to In 'n Out Burger. We'll go bowling." He strolled leisurely down the hall all the way to his room, talking over his shoulder.

When he crossed the threshold to his room he immediately kicked into high gear and began to get dressed. He knew that Montana was stressed about this job, but he wasn't sure why. Everything that she had told him so far had been strictly need to know. He knew that she was used to working alone, as was he, but she *asked him* to come in on this. She needed his help and she was still acting like she hadn't asked him for a favor. He was willing to give her space and let her have room to herself to prepare, but she needed to be fully aware of the fact that she was not going to into this alone. She needed to remember that he was there and not just when she needed to use him.

* * *

Montana pulled the Buick around to the back of the art gallery and parked near a dumpster. They had arrived there before anyone else. If any of the guests happened to see their car when they drove in, they more than likely would assume that it belonged to somebody who was working the party behind the scenes and ultimately ignore it.

They hid until sundown in the line of trees that surrounded the park. Like a repeat of the events at Fallingwater, they watched unmarked black vehicle after unmarked black vehicle pull into spots around the park. Business type men and prostitute type women exited the cars in pairs and large groups and stumbled laughing into Hollyhock House. Tripper watched through the dusky twilight as an especially brash prostitute was dragged, laughing like a Joker victim, into the building, hanging off the neck of a man in a three-piece suit.

"Your girlfriend's dead by the way," Montana spoke for the first time in hours, "may she rest in peace."

"Who?" Tripper made his confused old man Hank face.

"You're girlfriend. From Fallingwater. The box fan." Montana checked the time on a digital wristwatch Tripper had never seen before, then looked out over the lawn toward the house.

Tripper's head rocked back slowly in recognition. He had not thought about her in years. He hadn't thought about her since Montana pulled into the parking lot at the Doyle Hotel and Suites. The true meaning of what Montana was trying to insinuate finally sunk in and he shook his head in frustration.

"Fuck you, with the 'my girlfriend' shit," his voice was low but direct. "She may have been a sleaze, but she was still a kid."

"Wanna hear how she died?" Montana looked through a pocket-sized pair of binoculars.

"No. Wanna tell me?"

"She was stomped to death by a miniature Shetland pony."

Tripper made the face of a small child discovering that it didn't like the taste in its mouth. "Can't say I saw it ending that way."

"Yeah, about three years ago. I ran into her at another party thrown by our friends here. They had hired her to fuck horse."

"How the hell do you get stomped to death by a horse that size? It's like the size of a Power Wheels jeep."

"Apparently, it didn't take too kindly to her imitation of a dying Lasko. Spooked it. She was too stoned to realize it. Little bastard caved her face in."

"Jesus."

"I guess it had a cold or something, too. It kept sneezing fountains, literal fountains of pistachio green pudding everywhere. The place was a mess."

"You're fucking with me."

Montana held up her free hand into a Girl Scout salute. "Scouts honor."

"Why the hell are you telling me all of this? Now?"

"It's not fun being fucked with right before a job, is it?" Montana pulled her eyes away from the binoculars and shot them at Tripper.

Tripper had had enough. "Ok, first of all, fuck you. You've done nothing but ignore me this whole trip. I came with you, because you somehow managed to convince me back in *Michigan* that you needed my help. You evaded talking to me for almost thirty-six *straight* hours, you spent all day in your bedroom and then come out expecting me to hop to it, but you've never told me why you needed me in the first place. I'm really starting to wonder how much you needed help on this job and how much you just felt like fucking with me some more. And right now, I am about ten seconds away from saying fuck it, walking off this hill, giving away your position and flying the fuck back to Lansing."

Montana gently bit her lip and looked down at the ground. It was hard for Tripper to see her face in the fading light but there was enough to tell that her normally pale cheeks were flushed.

"I told you I was hard to get along with," her voice was low and disarming. "If you want to leave you can, I won't blame you. Just please do it quietly."

The wave of rage that washed up inside Tripper began to roll back. "I just want you to talk. Tell me what you know. I came with you to help. I'm here to help. But I, just like you, need to know what the hell I'm flinging myself in to."

Montana barely waited for him to finish speaking. "It's gotten worse. There used to be rules, now there aren't any rules. The old guard is leaving, and the new kids are coming up and they have no clue what they're doing. It's dangerous. More dangerous than it was before, and I know enough about myself to know that I can't do this on my own anymore. If I do, I'm going to wind up dead. And I'll be just another dead Guild member and a notch in their belt." Montana paused, looked up from her hands and back at Hollyhock. "I know that you're still mad at me and I have a lot of time to make up for, but I thought that an act of faith like this, my faith in you and whatever faith in me you have left...it might help us form a stronger bond and we'd be able to pick up where we left off. I had my eye on you to recruit you since you started at ISE. Then you wound up getting a job at LMJ and there was reason for our paths to cross and everything fell into place. But I didn't expect for you to have any sort of interest in me. And at the time it made me a little bit uncomfortable. To be honest I'm still a little bit uncomfortable with it now. That morning in my hotel room you seemed very...insistent."

"I know someone like that."

"I thought that with time, it might go away but apparently it didn't. I meant what I said on the ride here, I'm not attracted to you. But it's nothing personal; I'm not attracted to anyone."

"I'd be surprised if you were."

"What's that supposed to mean?"

"I can't imagine you with anybody. You are a solitary unit. Even being partnered with you myself it seems a little awkward."

"I need you to know that no matter how you feel about me, you're not going to change me. Just like I'm not going to be able to change you. Think whatever you want to think about me; just don't include me in on it. And please try not to stare at me so much."

"That was mildly insulting, Montana, but I again thank you for your honesty."

Montana looked confused at his last statement.

"And try not to stare at *me* so much," he added. "Know what, no, keep doing it. I like your eyes, too."

Montana recognized his chess move and set her jaw. She held out her stiff hand to shake. "Truce?"

Tripper wrapped his warm hand around her cold hand and looked her in the eye with what he imagined to be Montana-like intensity. "Friends." He let the word hang there for a moment as he stared at her.

They had another conversation. This one was quiet, spoken only in stares. After a moment or two they let go of each other and turned back toward the house.

CHAPTER SIXTEEN

Blue Orchid/Party of Special Things to Do

John Denver's *Rocky Mountain High* spilled out of Hollyhock and down the hill to Hollywood Boulevard. Tripper and Montana slinked across the lawn toward the dry moat with their guns drawn. They moved like a SWAT team, one person moving and the other acting as cover until, they pressed up against the wall of the house. A motion sensitive light kicked on and illuminated the empty pool and the yard beyond. Tripper followed the path of the light across the cement pool, along the grass, up to the horizon and the lights of Los Angeles. He glanced down at Montana as she worked the door's lock with some sort of device that flashed red and green.

There suddenly was an eerie sound somewhere close to them. A carefree whistling that carried across the lawn and bounced off the empty cement, echoing like an amphitheater. Tripper finally recognized that it was the theme to *Penn & Teller: Bullshit!*. He lifted his weapon and scanned around the yard to find the source.

"Tripper," Montana whispered.

"Listening," Tripper searched the edge of the darkness for shadows.

"*Thank* you."

"What?" he looked down at her expecting to see the door open.

"You were whistling," she said still working the device.

"No, I wasn't," he said defensively.

The device beeped three times in quick succession and the door made a hollow metallic *click*. Montana stared directly at Tripper and stood up, tucked the device in a pocket in the inside back of her jacket and then pulled her Glock from her shoulder holster.

Tripper dropped his head then looked back out over the lawn. "Sorry."

John Denver echoed up and down the sand colored halls of Hollyhock as they slid into the beige living room. The room seemed somewhat vaguely Japanese in its overall design, but the furniture and wood accents were distinctly American. Montana and Tripper crept the length of the living room. staying close to the walls but far away from each other on opposite sides of the room. Tripper was unable to tell if Montana's footsteps were completely void of sound or if the music was loud enough that they were drowned out. Either was possible. His boots clopped and shuffled over the floor and stopped when he pressed himself against the wall. As they moved, the song switched to *Woman* by Wolfmother with the subtlety of a bullwhip. Tripper stumbled at the sudden change and felt like he was going to slide off the Earth. Montana maintained pace and reached the main entrance to the living room a few steps before him. They both stared at the floor and listened for which direction the music was coming from. After a moment or two they looked up at each other and gestured their heads in the same direction, toward the loggia. Montana took point and checked around the corner. She motioned with one hand for Tripper to follow.

Across the hall from the living room, a small set of stairs led down to tall, floor to ceiling glass doors that stood open, leading to a large grassy courtyard. On the opposite side of the courtyard, was a large rectangular pool buried beneath a seemingly hovering concert stage set up with lights and huge stacks. On the stage there was a man a little over six feet in height with long shaggy hair, white bunny ears, pants-less with red and white polka dotted boxers, a red silk kimono and a tight-fitting August Burns Red t-shirt jumping, kicking and strumming an air guitar along to the music. On either side of the stage were nude men in Pikachu mascot heads standing with their arms crossed. The gyrating man would occasionally run over to one of the men and furiously dry hump them as he held out his arms and flicked his tongue like an electrified iguana. In front of the stage, was a group of fifteen to twenty people in various mismatched costumes and states of undress who stood zombie-like, watching the stage.

Tripper and Montana waited in the doorway to the courtyard for a moment.

"What's our move here?"

"I was just trying to figure that out. There's not as many people here as there usually are, or as I thought there might be. Hopefully that should make things easier."

"Tripper Mayhew! Holy shit!" The voice echoed from the stage across the courtyard.

Tripper's eyes widened as he heard his name. He quickly raised his gun and pointed it in the direction of the stage. Montana slowly raised her gun as she looked at Tripper out of the corner of her eye, then gradually turned her head to face him. The man ran from his platform above the pool, across the courtyard, his red silk kimono flapping in the wind, stopping just in front of Tripper and Montana at the edge of the doorway. He was breathing was heavy and he sweating like it was his main profession. His irises were pinpoints and he ground his teeth as he spoke.

"What do you think of the music man Wolfmother kicks so much ass they never got the recognition they deserved that John Denver shit was my Dad's shit he used to play it every year we do it out of respect or something." The man's Dennis Hopper smile was deeply unsettling.

Tripper held his gun on the man and squinted his eyes, "What?"

"Tripper it's me remember Coda!" he exclaimed. He was far too excited.

Tripper slowly shook his head in stunned silence as he gradually aimed his gun toward the ground. Montana held her gun aimed at the man's chest, but was staring at Tripper.

"No. No, I don't remember."

"Coda man Coda Pembroke we worked together at LMJ a couple years ago!" Coda's smile was enormous and unyielding. His eyes darted between Tripper and Montana, waiting for someone to recognize him.

Tripper's faced bleached from the inside out and Montana's face jaw dropped. "Coda?" they said in unison.

"*Fuck* yeah man it's me who's this?" Coda's words came fast and articulated. His knees buckled for a moment and he quickly regained his balance.

Tripper was still stunned and, out of reflex, introduced Montana. Coda's eyes somehow managed to get wider upon hearing her name. He dug around in the pockets of his kimono before pulling out a joint and a lighter. He put the joint in his mouth and pointed at Montana with his lighter hand.

"Oh no shit you're the chick who was like kidnapped by clowns man the summer intern how's it goin' with that man did they hire you yet god damn it I am so fucking high!" He held the lighter up to his mouth and clicked it a few times before he could produce a flame.

"They went out of business, Coda." Tripper added calmly.

"Oh shit yeah I forgot how long ago was that?" Coda said blowing smoke as he talked.

"Five years," said Tripper scrunching his eyebrows together.

"Holy shit has it really been that fucking long god damn time just fucking flies by so are you guys like together now or something I mean you came together so did you like hook up and move out west---"

Red mist exploded from Coda's right shoulder and spattered all over Tripper and Montana. Tripper looked toward Montana who had regained her normal cold gaze.

"Woah-ly fuck did I just get shot?" Coda was on his back, upside down on the cement steps. He poked the bullet wound in his shoulder like a dead body.

Tripper looked from Coda to Montana, "How the hell did he know it was me? How the hell did he *see* me?"

Montana tucked her pistol into her shoulder holster and bent down to pick up his legs. "Help me pick him up."

Tripper glanced in the direction of the stage long enough to see the entire audience of people rushing for his end of the courtyard. He skipped down the steps and shoved his hands under Coda Pembroke's arms. Coda let out a sound somewhere between pain and excitement and, in his clueless drug haze, adjusted his body to help Tripper and Montana carry him. They shut and locked all the doors barely in time enough for the screaming, moaning crowd to reach them. Montana turned Coda to face out the glass doors and placed her boot in between his shoulders, pressing his face and chest against the glass.

"Ow man that's tender bro I think I got shot or something," Coda chuckled.

Montana aimed her gun at the back of Coda's head and addressed the people on the other side of the glass with her dagger stare. "The Barnsdall-Wright Agreement," she annunciated, "give it to us and Coda will live to fulfill his lifelong dream of being a hat mannequin."

A small dark man dressed in a red white court jester's costume spoke from the other side of the glass with a thick New Jersey accent. "The Barnsdall-Wright Agreement? I've heard about you Guild douche bags. You're not gettin' shit but hurt." He sneered as he spoke revealing a full set of yellow teeth to match the yellow of his eyes.

Montana looked him in the eye and lifted her gun, firing a round at the glass in the area right between the Jersey Jester's eyes. The round hit the glass with a crack before ricocheting off and grazing Tripper's left shoulder. Tripper stumbled and grabbed his shoulder with his weapon hand.

"What the fuck?"

Montana snapped her head in Tripper's direction with the slightest look of panic in her eyes. "Are you alright?"

"What the---what the fuck happened?"

"The glass is bulletproof, asshole," said the Jersey Jester. He stood bleeding from the forehead behind the glass, a giant smoke scorched patch of cracked glass in front of him. "Keep fuckin' shootin'. Maybe you'll take care of ya-selves for us."

"Shut the fuck up, Pogo."

Tripper looked up at Montana who had been staring at him this whole time.

"Are you ok?" she asked low.

"Yeah, I'm good. Thankfully I don't pass out at the sight of blood."

Tripper was suddenly reminded of the party at Fallingwater and hit the floor.

* * *

Tripper's eyes slowly opened as he felt the dry dusty California breeze blow across his face. He heard a muffled screaming and the sound of a man who, judging by his voice, was very ugly and enjoying himself way too much.

"Nurse Fistuala, give me a hand, here will you?" came the man's voice through the fuzzy dark.

They were playing *White Rabbit* again. Tripper let out a groan and tried to move his arms and legs. He wasn't surprised when he couldn't. When he finally opened his eyes, everything looked like it was upside down, because it was.

"One of my father's favorite tricks---," came Coda's voice from somewhere. It was much slower and measured now.

"Oh, Christ," mumbled Tripper.

"was to kill his enemies in way that it looked like they killed themselves. You eliminate someone who fucked you over and nobody suspects it was you."

Tripper heard Montana struggling somewhere to his left. When he turned, he saw an inverted image of her being tied to a large decorative pillar. Based on the way it moved, it was made of aluminum, but clearly must have been weighed down at the base.

"Do you wanna know how he did it?"

"Oh, please tell me," Tripper struggled to speak as he looked down his chest up at the sky. He could feel the blood rushing into his head with each heartbeat.

"Caffeine," Coda spoke with a smile in his voice.

Tripper stopped. His eyes widened as he remembered that rainy day at Shady Acres. He looked around frantically until he found Coda, sitting on the grassy ceiling on a large ornate red and gold throne, a California flag draped over his wounded shoulder like a blanket and the Jersey Jester standing at his side, leaning against the chair back.

"Caffeine?"

"Caffeine," Coda smiled again. "See, Dad didn't like energy drinks. He said that they were just cans of overpriced unsweetened pop. But Dad never drank one, so he didn't know the magic."

A large, hairy, half nude man stepped in front of Tripper, his dick almost pressed into Tripper's face. Tripper struggled to move and felt a sharp prick on the inside of his left arm.

"Then he found out that we kids, who were my and your age at the time, were drinking several of them in a row and dying of heart arrhythmia. So, he came up with the idea of injecting people with enough caffeine... that they would *die*. They'd leave a bunch of empty energy drink cans around and leave. And when the coroner would check the body, he would say, 'Oh, this kid just had too many energy drinks and killed himself.' It sounded pretty flimsy to me at the time, but I came to find out that the cops were in Dad's back pocket, so it made sense after a while but...what are you going to do."

The large hairy man stepped away from Tripper with a chuckle. He was wearing a black leather vest and an overly large black strap-on on his face like a Pinocchio nose. Standing next to him was a woman in an ill-fitting latex nurse costume, cut to expose her breasts. Even from an inverted position, Tripper could tell that behind her eyes she was gone.

"I'm sorry it had to end this way, Tripper," Coda said, not sorry at all. "We could have partied."

"Can you at least... grant me the dignity... to *not* die to a Jefferson Airplane song?" Tripper said, feeling like he was beginning to lose consciousness.

There was a very loud sound of meat hitting meat somewhere near Tripper and he saw a flash of light for a second. Almost instantly he could taste the blood in his mouth.

"Sweet dreams, baby boy. Keep that asshole tight for me, huh?" Strap-On Face pressed the strap-on against Tripper's face and leaned in close, pushing it aside. He pressed his tongue to Tripper's temple and in one long slow motion, licked up to Tripper's jaw line. Strap-On Face pulled back away from Tripper with a big smile, bearing the whitest, most crooked teeth Tripper had ever seen. He then hocked and spit in Tripper's face, rubbing it around and up his nose. Tripper shook his head and sputtered, suddenly less concerned with what was on the rubber dick and more concerned with what was in Strap-On Face's saliva. Tripper heard the sound of someone hocking and spitting again and shut his eyes. He heard the wet sticky *splat*, but didn't feel anything. Slowly he opened his eyes to see Strap-On Face with a mean look pointed in Montana's direction. A combination of mucus and saliva dripping off his large prosthetic phallus.

"How the fuck do *you* like it, you sissy bitch?" Montana said with an intensity Tripper had never heard before.

Strap-On Face stepped up to Montana and rubbed her face with the back of his hand. "Look at this mouth. Look at this sweet little mouth." He slapped Montana open handed through the face. She glared up at him. "I'll bet you take a lot of cock, huh, sweetie?" He began slapping her repeatedly through the face, each slap more forceful and intense than the last. "A lot of fucking cock in that sweet little fucking mouth." He pressed his forehead against hers and stared menacingly into her eyes, shoving the fake cock into her mouth and moving it in and out three times. "Well don't worry,

sweetheart. We're gonna blow you out like an after-Christmas sale."
He then pulled the strap-on out of her mouth and shoved his middle
and index fingers into her mouth with the same white crooked
toothed smile he gave Tripper.

Tripper wanted to say something about how stupid Strap-On
Face's last comment was, but he didn't want to piss him off and get
Montana hurt. Just then Montana bit down on Strap-On Face's fingers with everything she had and all the force she could summon
from her ancestors. Strap-On Face's eyes widened farther than he
thought was possible and he let out one long, continuous high-
pitched shriek. After about three seconds, Nurse Fistula came out
of her drug fog just enough to notice that something was wrong
and stared at Strap-On Face like Nipper the Victrola dog. The Jersey
Jester came running from his spot next to the throne and punched
Montana in the face with his weak noodle-y arms, just hard enough
to knock her head to the side and rip the fingers out of her mouth.
The Court Jester's sudden stop and then follow through was
enough to knock him off balance and send him tumbling into Tripper, yanking the i.v. out of his arm with a sharp painful jerk.

Tripper felt every tendon be ripped out of his arm as the i.v. was
pulled out, and shut his eyes for fear of what might fly into them.
There was a loud scuffle and Tripper heard Montana scream in anger
as the aluminum column fell to the ground. He turned his head toward the noise and was just beginning to open his eyes when he
heard a gunshot. There was great collective gasp, the kind that you
only hear in movies or large sporting events, then the sound of running footsteps on grass. Tripper was afraid to look.

"M-Montana?" he said softly.

He felt an icy cold hand press into his neck.

"Sh. It's me. Stay quiet. I'm gonna get you down."

Tripper opened his eyes again. All he could see was his heartbeat, so he decided to close them again. After about 10 seconds, maybe a couple of hours, his body slowly crumpled to the ground and he landed on his head.

"No, wait! Don't! Shit." Montana whispered behind him.

He felt the cool wet grass against the back of his neck. A rush of the warm air ran up his nose and danced around in his lungs.

"C'mon," Montana grunted as she knelt down and ducked her head under his shoulder, straining to lift Tripper to his feet. "You gotta work with me here."

Tripper's feet moved like he had a spinal injury. They spanned the fifteen feet from the scene of the incident, over to the cement sidewalk that surrounded the courtyard. Montana dropped Tripper to the ground and tipped over a six-foot long wooden folding table for them to take cover behind, knocking over store bought fruit and meat trays. Montana pressed Tripper's gun into his hand as he began to get feeling back in his arms and legs. It wasn't a feeling that he wanted to have. Every muscle in his body burned. He fought the urge to fall asleep.

"What... *the fuck* ...did you get me into?" he said doing his best to smile.

Montana looked over the table at the courtyard for any signs of movement. "I know, I'm sorry," she said hurriedly. "Let's just get you walking again and get the fuck out of here. I didn't think this would happen. And when it did, I didn't think that we would make it this far."

"No, it was pretty simple, actually. You just called that one guy a sissy bitch and then they fell apart like a god damn Jenga tower. They're a bunch of push-overs." Tripper rushed through what he was saying then shut his eyes tightly, biting his bottom lip. His legs felt like they were on fire just below the surface of his skin. He could feel sweat pouring down his face. He quickly wiped his forehead with one hand, then pressed it back into the ground to lift himself off the floor and take his weight off his legs. With his eyes still shut he heard Montana's panicked voice:

"Oh fuck, Tripper, are you alright?"

"Yeah, why?" He asked, trying to fake calm. He looked over at Montana whose wide blue eyes were looking at him terrified.

"You're bleeding."

Tripper went to wipe his face again and saw that his hand was covered in blood. He stared at his hand confused. "Is it bad?"

"It's all over your face," she said, frightened.

"Huh." He stared at his hand a moment more then pulled a grey paisley bandana out of one of the cargo pockets on his pants.

Montana leaned in toward Tripper and held his head in both hands. He could feel the cold steel of her Glock pressed against the side of his head. She investigated his eyes with the same EMT drive she had five years earlier when he was falling asleep in her hotel room. "Don't fucking fade on me now, Trip, look at me. Did you get shot?"

Tripper reeled from how fast and intense Montana was talking. "I don't think so. I think Slappy the Clown scraped me with the i.v. after he ripped it out of my arm."

"This is didn't come from a needle. This is cut is pretty deep," she said looking into his eyes.

"Oh, wait. Didn't that nurse bitch shoot at us after you bit off fuck-nut's fingers?"

"Look at me," she said insistently.

Tripper stopped moving and looked up at Montana.

"I think you have a concussion. How many fingers am I holding up?"

Just as she finished talking, they heard three shots rip by and hit the wall behind them. They both covered their heads and ducked. The shots echoed through the courtyard, then there was silence.

"Did you see where they came from?" Montana whispered.

"No," Tripper whispered back.

Montana slowly lifted her head and looked around. Once she established that the coast was clear, she tapped Tripper on the shoulder three times and he slowly sat up. Montana pressed her back against the wall and reached into her jacket, pulling out a silencer.

"Name all of the main and lesser functions of Trigonometry." Montana whispered quickly, attaching the silencer to her Glock.

Tripper sat holding the bandana over the gushing wound on his head. He closed his eyes and gritted his teeth, trying to fight the oncoming headache. "Sine...cosine. Tangent...cosine...Fuck me, do I have to name them all?" he whispered.

"Yes." Montana said looking around the corner. She said the word faster than Tripper had ever heard anyone say a single syllable word.

"Sine, cosine. Tangent, cotangent. Secant, cosecant." Tripper moved his head from side to side in time with his words.

"Good. Now name all of the drummers of Nirvana in chronological order." Montana moved, then suddenly became very still. Tripper couldn't tell what she was doing.

"Aaron Burckhard, Dale Crover, Dave Foster, Chad Channing, Dave Grohl." Tripper waited for her to respond. "Did I get it?" He started to become panicked and whispered hoarsely, "Montana?"

"Shh." It came out so quickly it sounded more like a sound effect than the drawn-out manner it is usually delivered.

They sat in silence for what felt like an eternity. Montana tracking an unseen target and Tripper trying to stop the bleeding. There
was a sound of shuffling feet on the other side of the courtyard.
Montana fired twice. The sound of a body hitting cement echoed
across the lawn. A bullet shot passed Tripper, almost grazing his
chest and just barely missing Montana's back. Tripper looked to his
left and fired across his chest into the dark.

"*Fuck...me*," Coda called out.

"Tag, you're it!" Tripper called back.

Montana spun around and stared at Tripper, her eyes wide with
anger. "What the fuck are you doing?"

"Just follow my play...back my lead...fuck it." Tripper pressed his
back and hands to the wall behind him and crab walked his way to
his feet. He stumbled his first few steps from behind the table before
he could regain his normal stride.

"Get down!" Montana whispered hoarsely from behind the
table.

"Alright, assholes...where the fuck are you, Coda? There you
are." Tripper flipped on his safety before gently tossing his Glock
into the air to readjust his grip and hold the barrel. "Let's see if you
are as big of a bitch as your Dad."

Tripper picked Coda up off the ground by the back of his t-
shirt and clocked him across the face with the butt of his gun. Coda
let out a brief groan then went limp. Tripper examined him for a

minute before dropping him face first on the ground. He put his boot on Coda's back aimed his gun at the back of his head.

"Alright, assholes, it's over. All this Fourth of July, Wright building shit, it's over. Done. If one of you fucktards doesn't hand either me or my associate the Kendall-Wright agreement---"

"Barnsdall-Wright agreement," Montana corrected. She was now standing in front of the table aiming her gun into the dark, slowly panning back and forth across the courtyard.

"Barnsdall-Wright agreement," Tripper corrected, "in the next thirty seconds, my associate and I are going to kill every last one of you and ship a box of your collective genitals to ISE headquarters in Utah. That's it. One. Two."

The courtyard was once again silent. Tripper looked over at Montana, who was looking back at him. Montana shrugged and shook her head. He looked down at Coda and noticed the dark red patch that had developed on the back of his silk kimono and stomped on it. Coda regained consciousness screaming.

"Three!" Tripper called out. "Four."

"We got it, we got it. Fuckin' douchebags." The Jersey Jester stumbled across the courtyard holding his face with one hand and carrying a fat manila envelope in the other. He made his way over to Tripper and extended the envelope to him. "Ya happy now, you fuckin' prick?"

Tripper smiled wide and nodded, "I am." He raised his gun and fired a single round into the Jester's face that entered his left eye and created a red cloud behind his head. "And getting happier by the minute."

Montana made her way over to Tripper, ever vigilant of who might be hiding in the shadows. "We good?" she asked low.

Tripper reached into the envelope and pulled out several pages, smearing them with blood. He tried to read them in the dark, before realizing that he had never done this before and didn't know what he was looking for.

"Uhh..."

Montana leaned over his shoulder and read the bloodstained paper by the light of the stage. "We're good," she said under her breath to him. "We're good!" Her voice echoed through the rear courtyard of Hollyhock.

"Love forty, schmucks." Tripper called out with a steely look, grinding his teeth. "Best start packing up, because as of right now, you are all *officially* trespassers."

CHAPTER SEVENTEEN

Padam Padam

Montana and Tripper pulled out onto Hollywood Boulevard and turned west. The hum of the electric engine and the sounds of the city were both loud and alien to them after the gunfight at OK Hollyhock. Tripper leaned out the window, spitting blood until they hit Normandie Avenue, then sat back in his seat and left the window rolled down. Montana would reach down and touch the canvas bag between them a couple of times a minute, like it was a kitten trying to escape. She sat nervously chewing her lip with one fang and nonchalantly checking her rearview. For it being the Fourth of July, things were pretty dead. That just made her more nervous.

She reached for the radio with her right hand, but her fingers wouldn't listen. After a couple of times she gave up and tried punching buttons with the first knuckle of her index finger. Tripper watched her endeavor with a blank expression before reaching out to the radio himself, causing Montana to instantly drop her hand.

"What d'you want on?" he asked plainly.

Montana ran her left hand through her hair nervously. "I don't know. Just something."

"You want Goulding?"

"I don't care. No."

Tripper had taken a lot of points from Montana in what little time he spent with her in the role of a Guild member, before he was abducted by clowns himself. He dressed like her, albeit in men's clothing, he carried a Glock in a shoulder holster on the left side under his jacket, and after every job he would go back to his room, take a shower and then crack open a bottle of whatever pop it was he was drinking that month and take the first sip while simultaneously turning on an album. That sort of dedication and discipline, even during downtime, was something that fascinated Tripper and he wanted to emulate it as much as possible.

He had tried a lot of music to come down to over the years, but he learned that the key was not to premeditate the music and just let his brain and body decide for him in the moment. That was what he did now, but unlike before, he had to take into consideration someone else's needs, and find something that could help both he and Montana come down. He sucked on his dry tongue and tasted a combination of blood and gun smoke. He scraped it across his two front teeth as he quickly flipped through his phone. Finally, he attached the phone to the magnetic connection on the dash and pressed play just as Montana hit the 101.

The car was filled with the magnificent and unearthly tones of Edith Piaf. Montana checked her side mirror and merged onto the expressway. They drove for about a quarter mile before Montana reached out and twisted the volume dial between the knuckles of her middle and forefinger, turning up the music. The trumpets blared through the small car and Edith's voice purred and hummed through the speakers. Montana pressed a button on the steering wheel and the top of the car slid back and disappeared into a compartment behind the back seat. Tripper had made the right choice.

He looked over at Montana and watched as she ran her fingers through her hair and slowly decompressed. Tripper sank down in his seat and looked straight ahead, the nocturnal skyline of southern California opening in front and above him. He looked up to the street lights that lined the expressway, the cold LED beams shooting down on what few drivers there were on the road. He took a deep breath through his nose and felt dried blood crack and break loose, followed by a warm rush of night air, gasoline and exhaust. Montana held her left hand up in the wind, catching it with her palm, her bloody scraped knuckles displayed for the world to see. The incessant ring of Tipper's headache began to sink into a low-level hum, before subsiding completely. Montana pulled back her shoulders and craned her neck to one side. Tripper glanced over one last time at Montana whose ice blue eyes were cutting through the blackness of the night, staring at some far-off location that no one, except her, could see. She softly mouthed the lyrics to herself; the stream of dried blood from her nose to her lip cracked and flaked off with each syllable. Over her head, to the west, way off in the distance, there were fireworks exploding somewhere near the Hollywood Bowl.

CHAPTER EIGHTEEN

How Far Can Too Far Go?

They got off on Lakeridge Road, circled around to Cahuenga Boulevard West, and followed it until they hit Highland Avenue, to exit back on to the Hollywood Freeway. It was somewhere around three in the morning before Montana and Tripper got back to the house on Deronda Drive. They needed the air.

Montana locked the canvas bag in the den safe and then made her way to the shower. Tripper stood outside on the patio and examined the fire pit for a considerable amount of time before he decided on lighting it. A police siren screamed a couple of miles away and a helicopter passed over the house with a searchlight. Montana had assured him that is was a good neighborhood. He could usually tell a bad neighborhood from a good one, but he didn't know shit about West coast cities.

As a result of his travel over the last several years working with the Guild, Tripper had gotten to experience life in towns all over the country, except for the west coast. He had learned how to quickly get his bearings on a city and learn its back roads and alleyways. True citizens use uncommon roads more than main roads. If he was going to blend in, he had to learn his way around and fast. His mind wandered to the Battle of Mogadishu and soldiers having to learn a city's layout and backdoors under incoming fire. Another police cruiser raced by in the distance, chirping its siren. Tripper had read somewhere once, that a person said during the Watts Riots the neighborhood didn't even resemble a place in America. More like some far-off war-torn country. The LA riots of 92. Rodney King. 'The shit is on fire show' as Henry Rollins once put it.

"That is the real LA," Tripper thought to himself. "Not Hollywood and movies and recording studios. Los Angeles is a town that shouldn't have ever happened, on the extreme edge of a country founded by law breakers and revolutionaries. The creamy nostalgic façade is a glamour that has worked for too long and despite all other incoming reports. There are good people down there and up here, I'm sure. But it's a shit show. New York is the heartbeat of America, which is why the country is dying. LA is the American dream, which is why it shouldn't exist."

Montana walked out onto the patio wearing a faded Smashing Pumpkins *Mellon Collie and the Infinite Sadness* shirt, sweatpants, and flip flops. Her hair was still damp and dripped onto the blanket thrown over her shoulder. Tripper followed her with his eyes as she set down her glass mug of London Fog on the arm of an Adirondack chair, then wrapped the blanket around her shoulders and sat down. She looked at the fire and slowly sipped her drink, her hair dripping softly onto the patio. Tripper looked back into the fire for a moment more before addressing Montana while staring at the flame.

"Pumpkins fan?" he said in an almost defensive tone.

"No," Montana said flatly. "I just like the shirt. I'd sooner listen to them than their rip-off band from Jersey, but that's not saying much."

"Fair enough. I thought we were going to have to stay at separate superhero hideouts there for a minute."

Montana stared into the fire with her ice blue eyes. Tripper could tell she was a million miles away. They sat in silence for a while, her staring at the fire and him, looking from the fire to her and back. She moved her lips occasionally as if she was speaking, but she made no noise. After a few times of this happening, Tripper finally asked her what she was saying. Montana spoke in her emotionless tone, never looking away from the fire.

"If it keeps on raining, the levee's gonna break." She slowly sipped her London Fog.

It was now Tripper's turn to stare into the fire as he spoke. "The levee done broke, the monkey got choked, and they all went to heaven in a little row boat, clap-clap."

"The levee hasn't broke," she said calmly. She turned toward Tripper and stabbed into him with her eyes. "But if it keeps on raining, it will."

Tripper had grown used to Montana's intensity, but the earnestness with which she spoke stopped him dead. The two locked eyes. The sound of the fire suddenly became very loud, as all other noises were sucked from the world.

"What do we do?" he asked. The words came out more panicked than he intended.

"We have to stop the rain."

"We're umbrellas."

"No. We have to stop the rain *entirely*."

"How the hell do you do that?"

Montana held her gaze on Tripper, burrowing her eyes into the back of his head. She tightened her mouth, the outline of her canines through her lips were illuminated by the fire light and exaggerated in the shadows. After a few moments, she looked away.

Tripper's body went cold. He was reminded of that morning at Fallingwater, when Montana shot the child molester who was asleep on the floor and his body slumped from a laying position. He hadn't realized how satisfied he was with their achievement that evening until she dropped the weight of the world on his shoulders. Their accomplishment had gone from a historic event, to a lone X scratched on the side of a fighter plane. Something inside of his head creaked then popped.

"Do you know what the Guild logo is?" Montana asked, staring into the fire.

"It's a snake eating its tail," Tripper said, thankful that he could accomplish something in responding to her question.

"It's Ouroboros reversed. Do you know what the motto is?"

"I didn't know there was one."

"Life is Pointless." She took a drink as she looked into the fire.

Tripper stared at Montana out of the corner of his eye as he mulled it over. "That's a little bleak, don't you think?"

"It's honest."

"How so?"

"What difference does it make what we do with our lives? We could both hang it up right now, go inside and never take a case again. Spend the rest of our lives eating... *Cheetos* and watching TV. What would it matter? We're both going to die. We don't have to do this to ourselves. We could make our lives much easier."

"But what about the levee?"

"What about the levee?"

"It's gonna break."

"It will break whether we are here or not. Neither of us could have been born and the world would be in the same state it's in now. The lives of two people have no effect on the world. They're not even a blip on the radar."

"What about the Guild? There's what 300, 350 members?"

"In a country of 321.4 *million*? How big of an impact do you think we could have?"

Tripper's gaze had slowly moved toward the heart of the fire. He glanced back over at Montana who was once again staring at him.

"Why do you do this then?" Tripper's voice was almost subsonic.

Montana leaned in conspiratorially toward Tripper; her normal icy standoffish visage completely disappeared. "Because I couldn't *live* with myself *otherwise*."

Tripper sighed so deeply he felt as if his chest would collapse. Montana searched his eyes for some sort of recognition. Once she found it, she began pulling Tripper ashore.

"Life is, by and large, pointless, Tripper. Rape, murder, disease, war, child molestation, battery, psychological abuse, physical abuse, Taylor Swift. If there ultimately was point, or a goal, or a finish line to life, do you think any of these things would be allowed to exist? And if they were, would they happen with such frequency and intensity? That's because there is no point, Tripper. These are all symptoms of terrified people scrambling for a life preserver because at some point in their lives they realized that they would die. And everything that they have done in their lives one day won't matter. It takes a lot less effort to be sadistic and cruel than it does to offer a helping hand. There's no point to life, Tripper. There's no grand scheme. No grand plan. We are all scrambling around over top of each other until we die. It is up to *us* to give our lives meaning. And that choice is unique and important to you and you alone. I'm sorry if I cracked any sense of cosmic good you felt in being a member, Trip. But it had to be done. If you're going to do this job you have to do it for yourself. That has always been the point of the Guild, though never explicitly stated. We are a group of wildly diverse people with one common interest; we want to do some good while we're here, before we get sucked into the yawning maw of the galactic Cuisanart. Everyone on this team is doing what they are doing for themselves, but they see the same desire in each other that they see in themselves, the desire to do good. Life is pointless, so do what feels right to you and get out of it what you can. That's it."

As she said her last words, a smile came across her face. It was a type of smile that Tripper had never seen her give before. It was one of true happiness. Her smile met her piercing blue eyes and exposed her pointy canines, both flashing and glittering in the fire-light. Tripper smiled too, but his was much more reserved. It was the smile of a man who had just been resuscitated on an operating table. But his joy was just as pure and thorough as hers.

* * *

Tripper and Montana awoke the next morning around the same time, both now finally feeling the full effect of wounds they had sustained the previous evening. Tripper was walking a little bit bow-legged and limping on his right foot. Montana compulsively stretched her back and shoulders, grimacing in pain and hissing through her teeth as she did it. It was still early when Tripper stumbled out of his room and into the kitchen, but Montana had beaten him there. She sat on a stool eating avocado toast off a plate on the island as she looked out the sliding glass doors in the back of the house, watching the sun come up. She did not react when Tripper came into the room.

"I was going to make you some, but I didn't want it to get cold," she said absently.

Tripper was touched, but masked most of his true emotions, revealing only a slight smile. "Thank you. I appreciate the thought."

He made his toast with the ingredients she left for him and the two ate in silence as they both looked out at the sun. Unable to sit comfortably, Tripper decided to stand as he ate. He hadn't wrapped his ankle before getting out of bed, so he stood on his left leg to take the weight off his right foot. Tripper was almost done with his breakfast when Montana finally spoke.

"You can talk, you know. Just because I'm not doesn't mean you don't have to."

"I know. I just don't have anything to say."

Montana looked at him incredulously. "No? Nothing at all. Nothing comes to mind you want to address?"

Tripper raised his eyebrows, shaking his head slightly. He looked from her, down at this plate and back at her. "Nope."

Montana turned back toward the patio window. She watched for a couple minutes before she picked up her plate and took it to the sink. After she cleaned up, Tripper stayed in the kitchen for a few minutes more. He looked over at where she had been sitting. It now looked as if no one had ever been there. The room felt cold and empty. He could hear Montana moving around somewhere deep in the house. He quickly cleaned up his plate and the utensils, then went to his room to start packing.

Tripper dragged his duffel bag out into the living room and dropped it on the floor next to Montana's; the white canvas bag with the ISE logo rested on top of it. Montana was sitting on the arm of a couch flipping through her phone. She bore her expression of deep thought; her eyes were wide and alert, her mouth slightly open exposing her fangs. Tripper made an attempt to sit down on the couch directly across from her, but ultimately wound up three quarters laying on his back, giving the illusion that he had either never known how to sit, or just gave up trying all together.

"Where are you off to?" he asked.

"Field office in Temecula," Montana replied deep in her phone. "I have to file my report about Hollyhock and then after that I think their sending me to Savannah. Some engineering and machine shop outfit."

She finished her sentence as if she were about to start another one. Tripper stared at her, waiting for her to add to her story, but she never did. He finally looked away from her and out the front window in the living room. A lone car drove by at a leisurely speed, blaring the radio at a level far too obnoxious for that time of the day.

"How 'bout you?" she finally said, still going through her phone.

"I gotta head to LAX. Need to catch a flight to Spokane, I think. Same sort of job I was doing in Lansing. Hopefully they don't have a pool. Be nice to get out of the Midwest for a while."

"Hey, I'm from the Midwest."

"Really? Where?"

"You weren't far from it. Water Township. Just a little bit outside Pontiac."

"Hmm," Tripper trailed off into deep thought. For some reason the idea that Montana came from somewhere seemed both strange and fascinating. After a moment or two he finally spoke. "Why did your parents name you Montana if you're from Michigan?"

"Why did your parents name you Tripper if you're from Earth?"

"I've asked them that question a lot. I've never gotten a straight answer."

Montana stood up and slipped her phone into an inside jacket pocket. Tripper tried to get up as quickly as her, but was slowed down by harsh, painful reality. Montana's ever cold and piercing eyes watched him like an unfortunate dog.

"You alright?" she asked plainly, when he finally stood up.

"Yeah, why?" he replied, trying to be funny.

Montana stared at him blankly. Tripper slowly made his way over to her and stopped about three feet away. They stood silently, staring awkwardly at each other.

"Can I hug you, or will I face a Federal indictment?" he asked, sounding a little bit defeated.

Somewhere in mid blink, Montana shot over to Tripper and squeezed him as hard as she could. Tripper's eyes widened, and he stumbled for a moment, before wrapping his arms around her and squeezing back. Montana let out a soft noise that sounded like something between a purr and a whimper. Tripper squeezed her a little bit tighter and nuzzled his face into her hair.

"I can't begin to thank you for helping me last night. And I'm sorry I almost got us killed," she finally said, a slight tear in her voice.

Tripper held on to Montana and swayed slightly, resting his head on top of hers. "It's alright. I'm glad I could help."

"It means a lot," she said. Her voice squeaked a little bit as she held back tears. "I'm not a cold, unfeeling robot arm."

"I never seriously thought you were. Just answer a god damn e-mail every once in a while, ok?" he said, trying to inject a little humor.

Montana hung onto him again for a moment, before pulling back as quickly as she had moved forward. Her face was a little flushed and her icy blue eyes were rimmed with red, her cheeks mildly moist from tears that made it through the bulwarks. She was not open to humor. Everything she was saying was dead serious.

"Ok," she said, wiping her face with one hand and regaining composure. "I will. I promise."

Tripper felt like he needed to say something. He didn't know how she would react, but he took a chance and did it anyway. With his right hand, he reached out and gently touched her shoulder. He knelt down a little bit, he didn't know why. Something he learned as a kid that people did when they were conveying serious information. "It's fine. I'm ok. You're ok. Don't get upset and beat yourself up about it. We're good. We made it."

Montana looked up at Tripper and directly in the eye. She stood quietly as she listened. When he finished speaking, she took a few moments to digest everything.

"Don't think I didn't notice what you did to my hair just there," she said, instantly shifting back into her normal self. "Just because I let that happen. It's still the same between us. I'm your friend. And that's all."

"And I'm still fine with that," Tripper said with a smile.

* * *

Tripper waved goodbye to Montana as she pulled out of the driveway and took off down Derado Drive. The smell of her hair was still in his nose. He had called for a car that, if the tracking system was to be believed, would be there in about ten minutes. Tripper put in his headphones, flipped through his phone and pressed play on *L.A. Woman*, then looked out at the sun hanging high over the Los Angeles basin. It wasn't what he hoped it would be, and it wasn't what they said it would be. It was, however, exactly what he thought it would be. Planes roared over head, backlit by the Eastern sun over the Western city and he was reminded of home. Reminded of the houses, apartments, schools and offices he had spent so much time in over the first quarter century of his life and how, right now, there was probably a plane screaming over the rooftops of those buildings, too. He had made it to the other side of the country, but he hadn't really gone that far.

Lightning Source UK Ltd.
Milton Keynes UK
UKHW020430030720
365951UK00012B/636